#5

MY BOYFRIEND IS A MONSTER
I Date Dead People

OR

MY BOYFRIEND IS SO TRANSPARENT

OR

MY SO-CALLED AFTERLIFE

OR

YOUR MEMORY STILL HAUNTS ME

OR

SOUL MATES

OR

I LOVE BOO

ANN KERNS

Illustrated by JANINA GÖRRISSEN

GRAPHIC UNIVERSE · MINNEAPOLIS · NEW YORK

STORY BY
ANN KERNS

ILLUSTRATIONS BY
JANINA GÖRRISSEN

WITH ADDITIONAL INKS BY
MARC RUEDA

LETTERING AND COVER COLORING BY
ELDON COWGUR

Copyright © 2012 by Lerner Publishing Group, Inc.

Graphic Universe™ is a trademark of Lerner Publishing Group, Inc.

Graphic Universe™
A division of Lerner Publishing Group, Inc.
241 First Avenue North
Minneapolis, MN 55401 U.S.A.

Website address: www.lernerbooks.com

Main body text set in CC MildMannered 7/7.5.
Typeface provided by Comicraft/Active Images.

Library of Congress Cataloging-in-Publication Data

Kerns, Ann, 1959–
    I date dead people / by Ann Kerns ; illustrated by Janina Görrissen.
        p. cm. — (My boyfriend is a monster ; #5)
    Summary: The renovation of Nora's old Victorian house unearths a teenaged poltergeist who falls in love with Nora, causing more ghosts to appear and Nora's parents to become quite unhappy.
    ISBN: 978–0–7613–6007–0 (lib. bdg. : alk. paper)
    1. Graphic novels. [1. Graphic novels. 2. Ghosts—Fiction. 3. Dating (Social customs)—Fiction. 4. High schools—Fiction. 5. Schools—Fiction.] I. Görrissen, Janina, ill. II. Title.
PZ7.7.K46Iam 2012
741.5'973—dc23   2011021542

Manufactured in the United States of America
1 – BC – 12/31/11

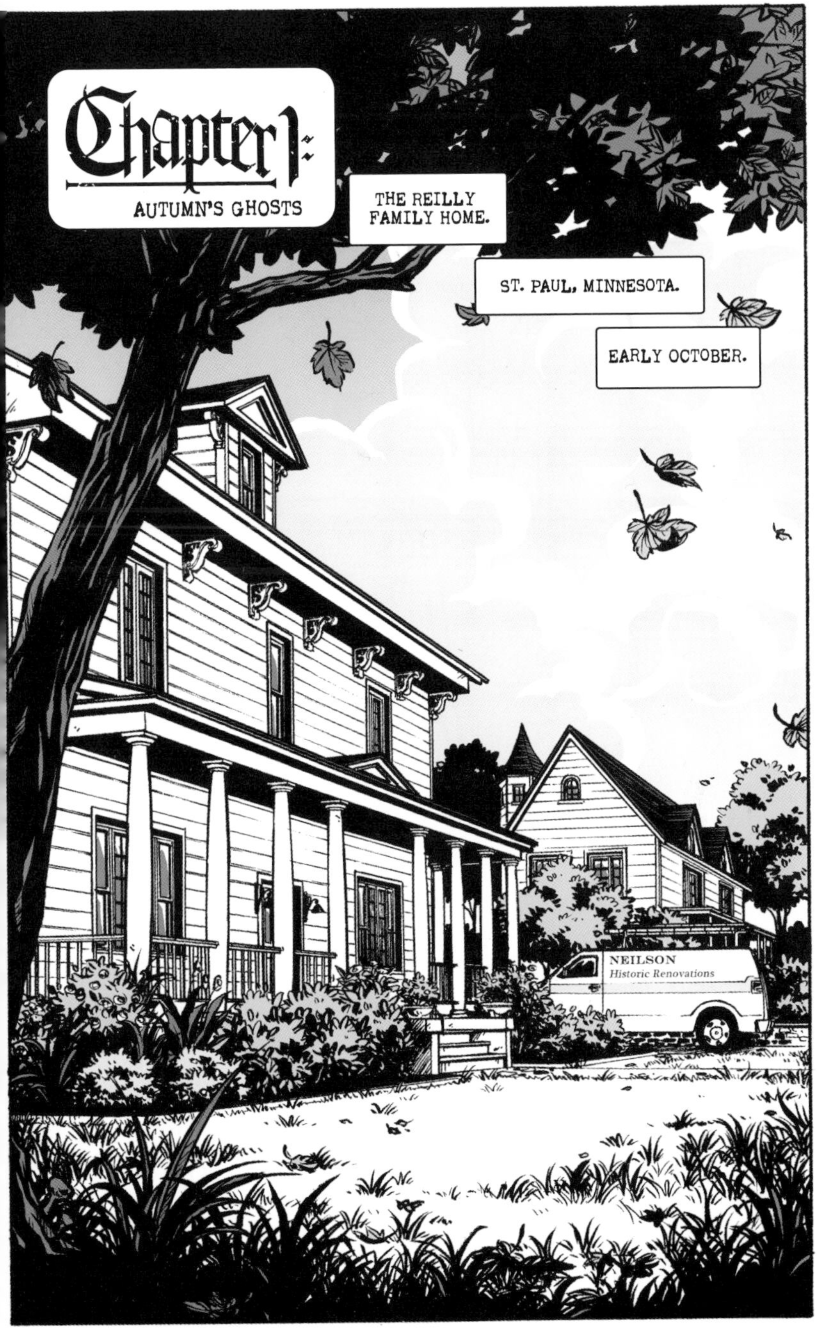
Chapter 1:
AUTUMN'S GHOSTS
THE REILLY FAMILY HOME.
ST. PAUL, MINNESOTA.
EARLY OCTOBER.
NEILSON
Historic Renovations

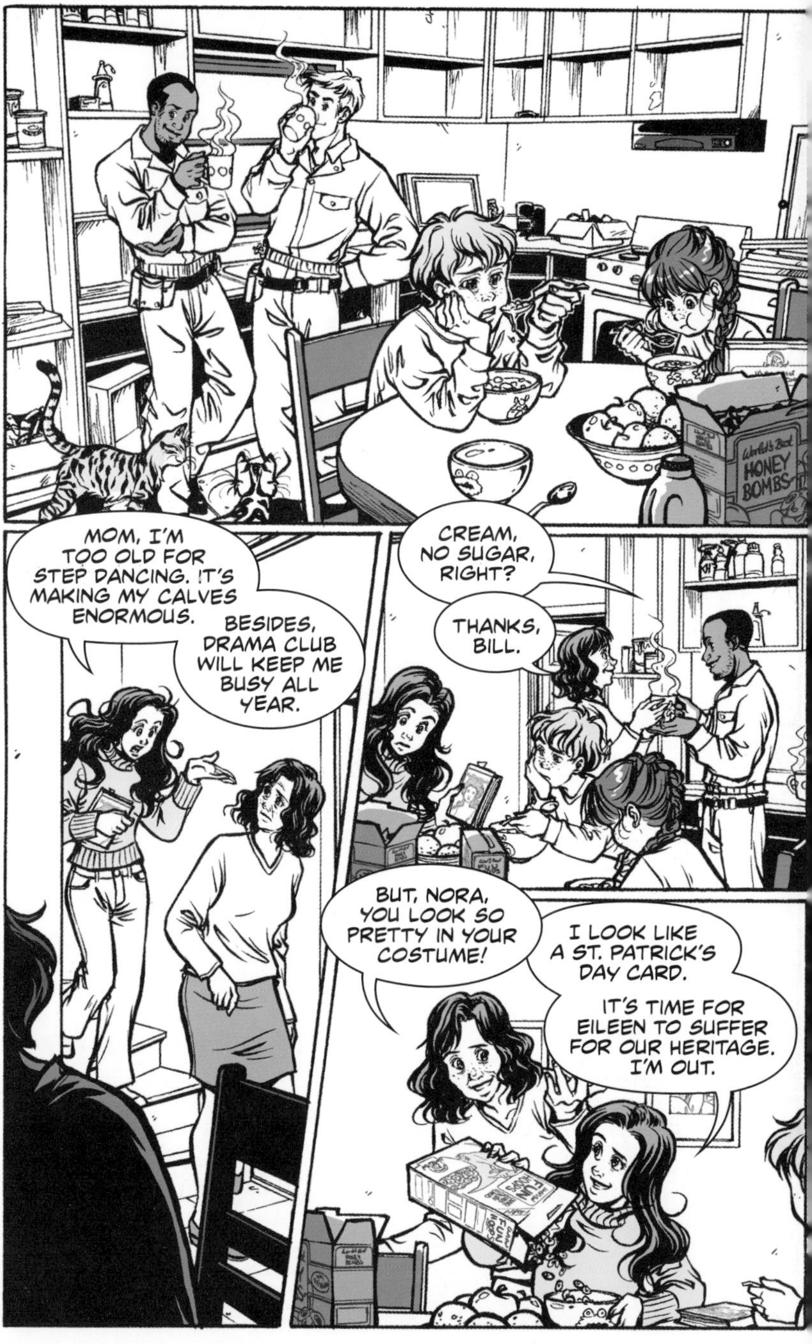

MOM, I'M TOO OLD FOR STEP DANCING. IT'S MAKING MY CALVES ENORMOUS.
BESIDES, DRAMA CLUB WILL KEEP ME BUSY ALL YEAR.
CREAM, NO SUGAR, RIGHT?
THANKS, BILL.
BUT, NORA, YOU LOOK SO PRETTY IN YOUR COSTUME!
I LOOK LIKE A ST. PATRICK'S DAY CARD.
IT'S TIME FOR EILEEN TO SUFFER FOR OUR HERITAGE. I'M OUT.

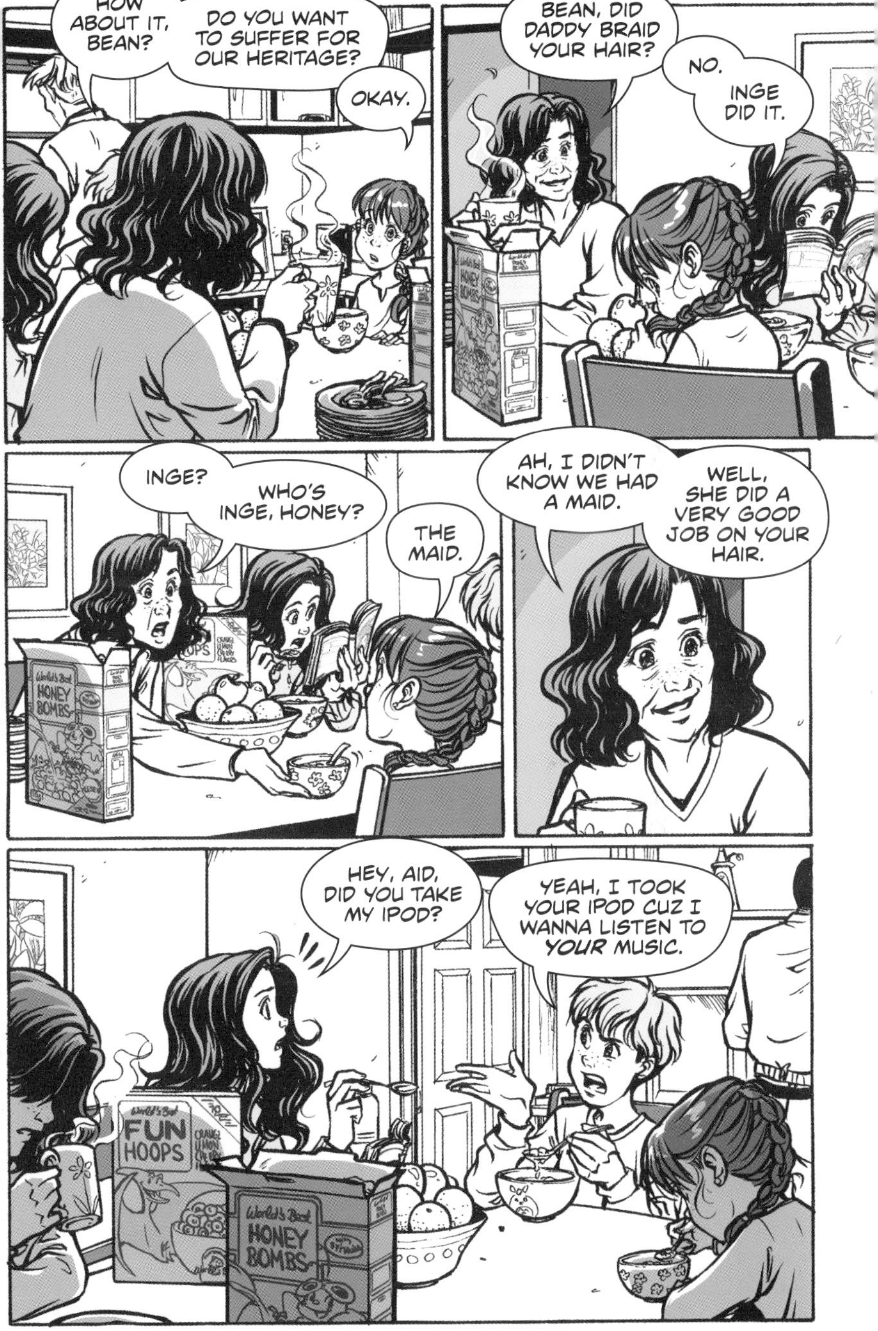
HOW ABOUT IT, BEAN?
DO YOU WANT TO SUFFER FOR OUR HERITAGE?
OKAY.
BEAN, DID DADDY BRAID YOUR HAIR?
NO.
INGE DID IT.
INGE?
WHO'S INGE, HONEY?
THE MAID.
AH, I DIDN'T KNOW WE HAD A MAID.
WELL, SHE DID A VERY GOOD JOB ON YOUR HAIR.
HEY, AID, DID YOU TAKE MY IPOD?
YEAH, I TOOK YOUR IPOD CUZ I WANNA LISTEN TO *YOUR* MUSIC.

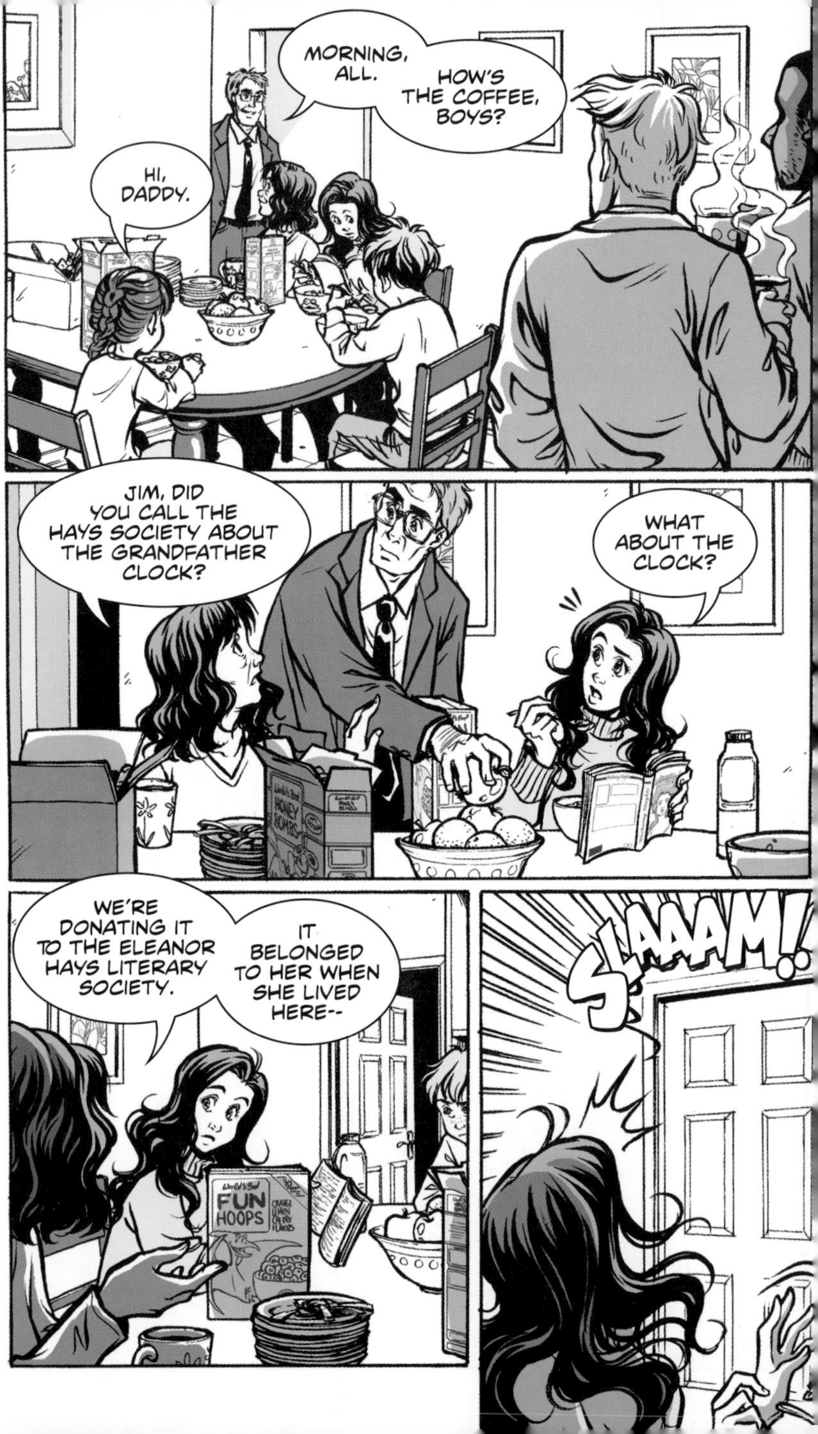
MORNING, ALL.
HOW'S THE COFFEE, BOYS?
HI, DADDY.
JIM, DID YOU CALL THE HAYS SOCIETY ABOUT THE GRANDFATHER CLOCK?
WHAT ABOUT THE CLOCK?
HONEY BOMBS
WE'RE DONATING IT TO THE ELEANOR HAYS LITERARY SOCIETY.
IT BELONGED TO HER WHEN SHE LIVED HERE--
FUN HOOPS
SLAAAM!!

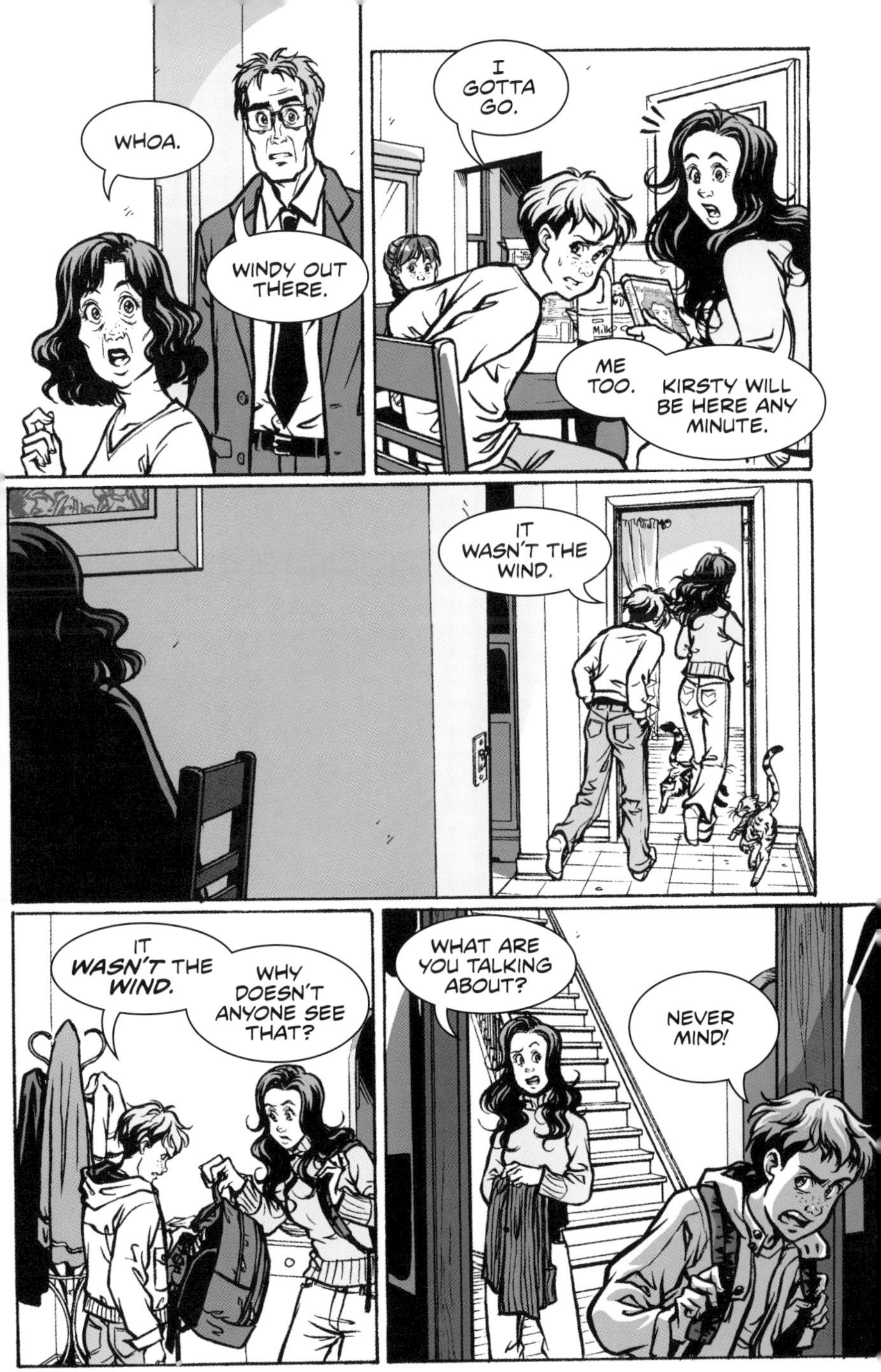
WHOA.
WINDY OUT THERE.
I GOTTA GO.
ME TOO.
KIRSTY WILL BE HERE ANY MINUTE.
IT WASN'T THE WIND.
IT *WASN'T* THE *WIND.*
WHY DOESN'T ANYONE SEE THAT?
WHAT ARE YOU TALKING ABOUT?
NEVER MIND!

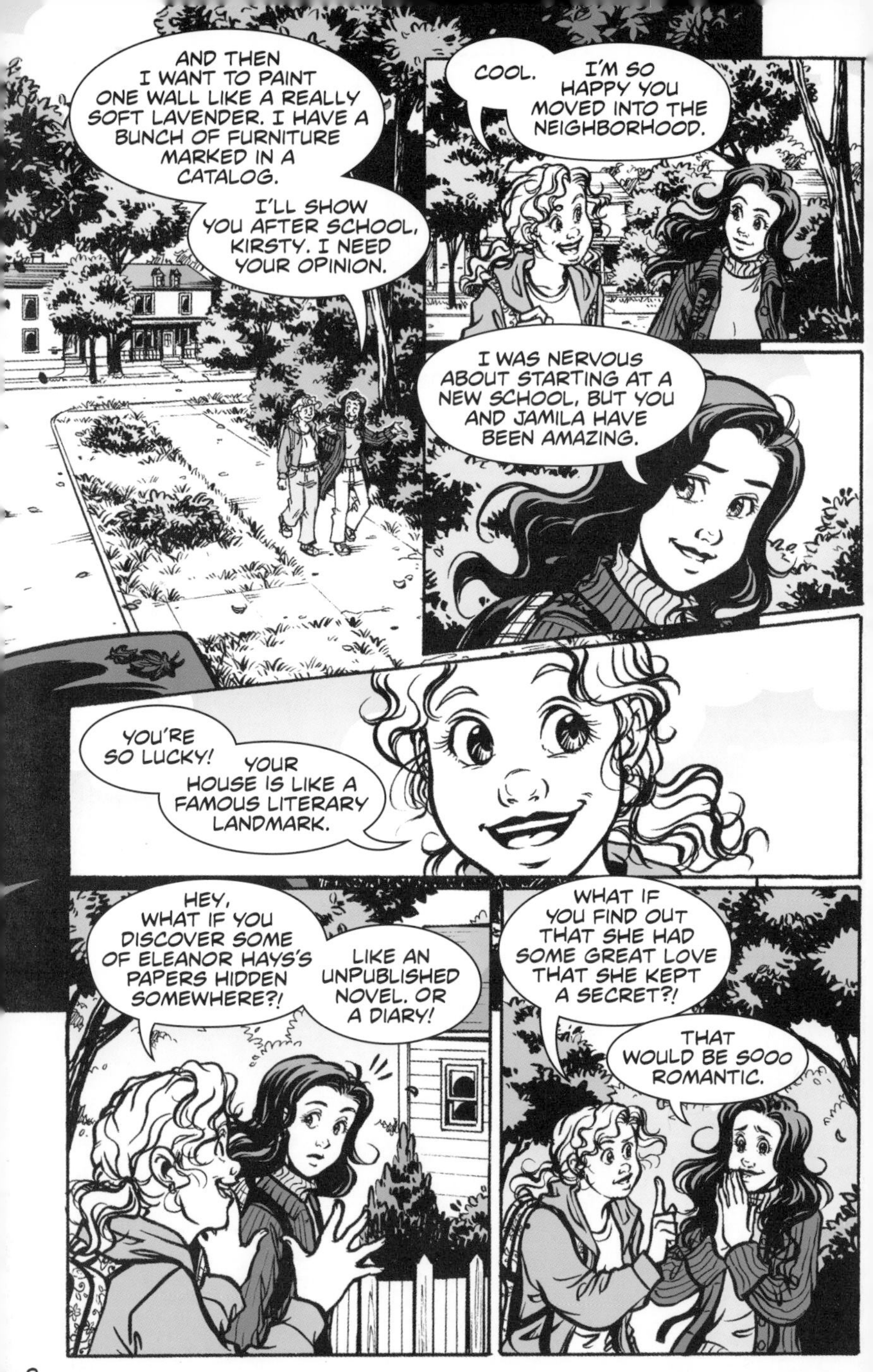
AND THEN I WANT TO PAINT ONE WALL LIKE A REALLY SOFT LAVENDER. I HAVE A BUNCH OF FURNITURE MARKED IN A CATALOG.
I'LL SHOW YOU AFTER SCHOOL, KIRSTY. I NEED YOUR OPINION.
COOL.
I'M SO HAPPY YOU MOVED INTO THE NEIGHBORHOOD.
I WAS NERVOUS ABOUT STARTING AT A NEW SCHOOL, BUT YOU AND JAMILA HAVE BEEN AMAZING.
YOU'RE SO LUCKY!
YOUR HOUSE IS LIKE A FAMOUS LITERARY LANDMARK.
HEY, WHAT IF YOU DISCOVER SOME OF ELEANOR HAYS'S PAPERS HIDDEN SOMEWHERE?!
LIKE AN UNPUBLISHED NOVEL. OR A DIARY!
WHAT IF YOU FIND OUT THAT SHE HAD SOME GREAT LOVE THAT SHE KEPT A SECRET?!
THAT WOULD BE SOOO ROMANTIC.

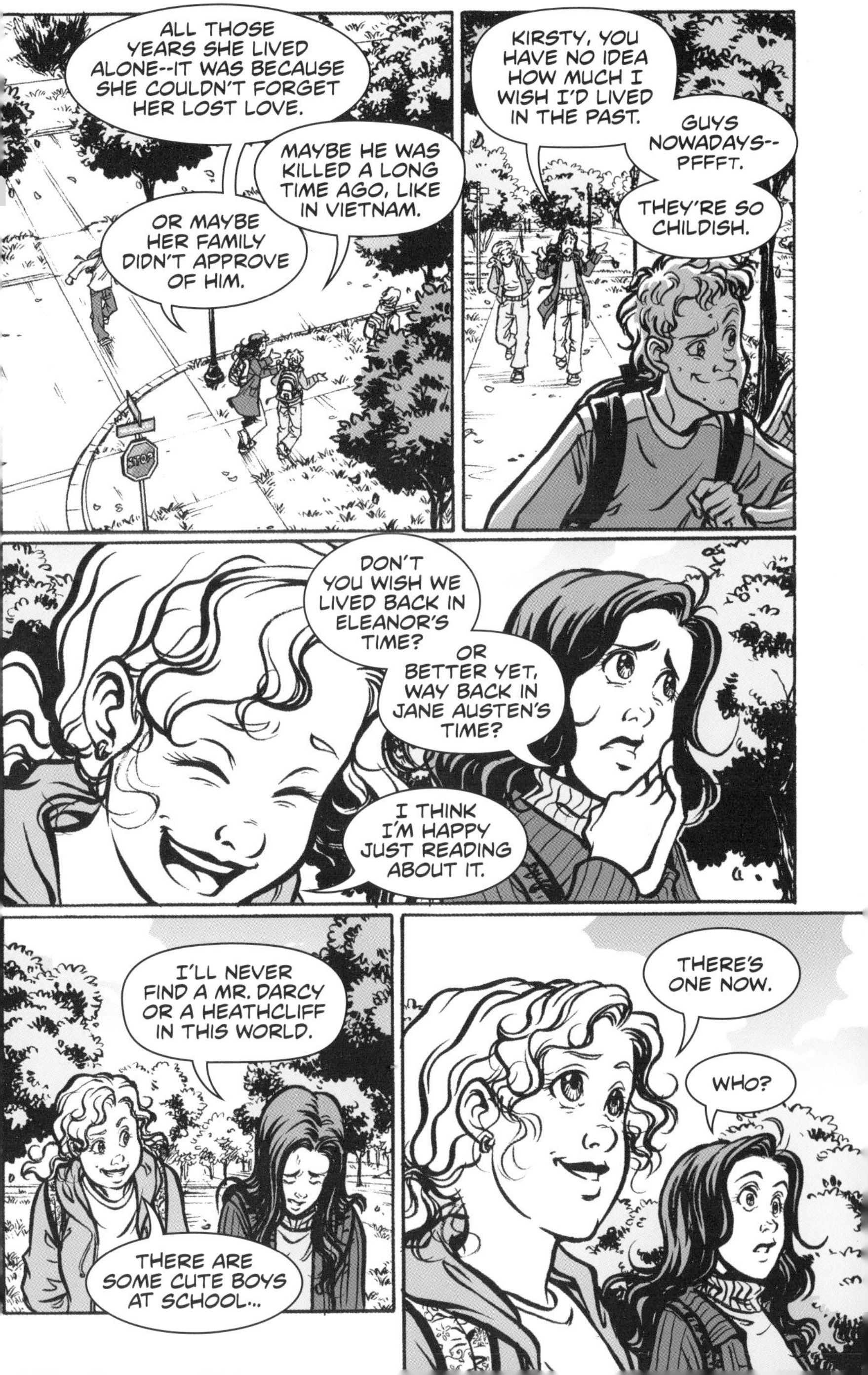
ALL THOSE YEARS SHE LIVED ALONE--IT WAS BECAUSE SHE COULDN'T FORGET HER LOST LOVE.
MAYBE HE WAS KILLED A LONG TIME AGO, LIKE IN VIETNAM.
OR MAYBE HER FAMILY DIDN'T APPROVE OF HIM.
STOP
KIRSTY, YOU HAVE NO IDEA HOW MUCH I WISH I'D LIVED IN THE PAST.
GUYS NOWADAYS-- PFFFT.
THEY'RE SO CHILDISH.
DON'T YOU WISH WE LIVED BACK IN ELEANOR'S TIME?
OR BETTER YET, WAY BACK IN JANE AUSTEN'S TIME?
I THINK I'M HAPPY JUST READING ABOUT IT.
I'LL NEVER FIND A MR. DARCY OR A HEATHCLIFF IN THIS WORLD.
THERE ARE SOME CUTE BOYS AT SCHOOL...
THERE'S ONE NOW.
WHO?

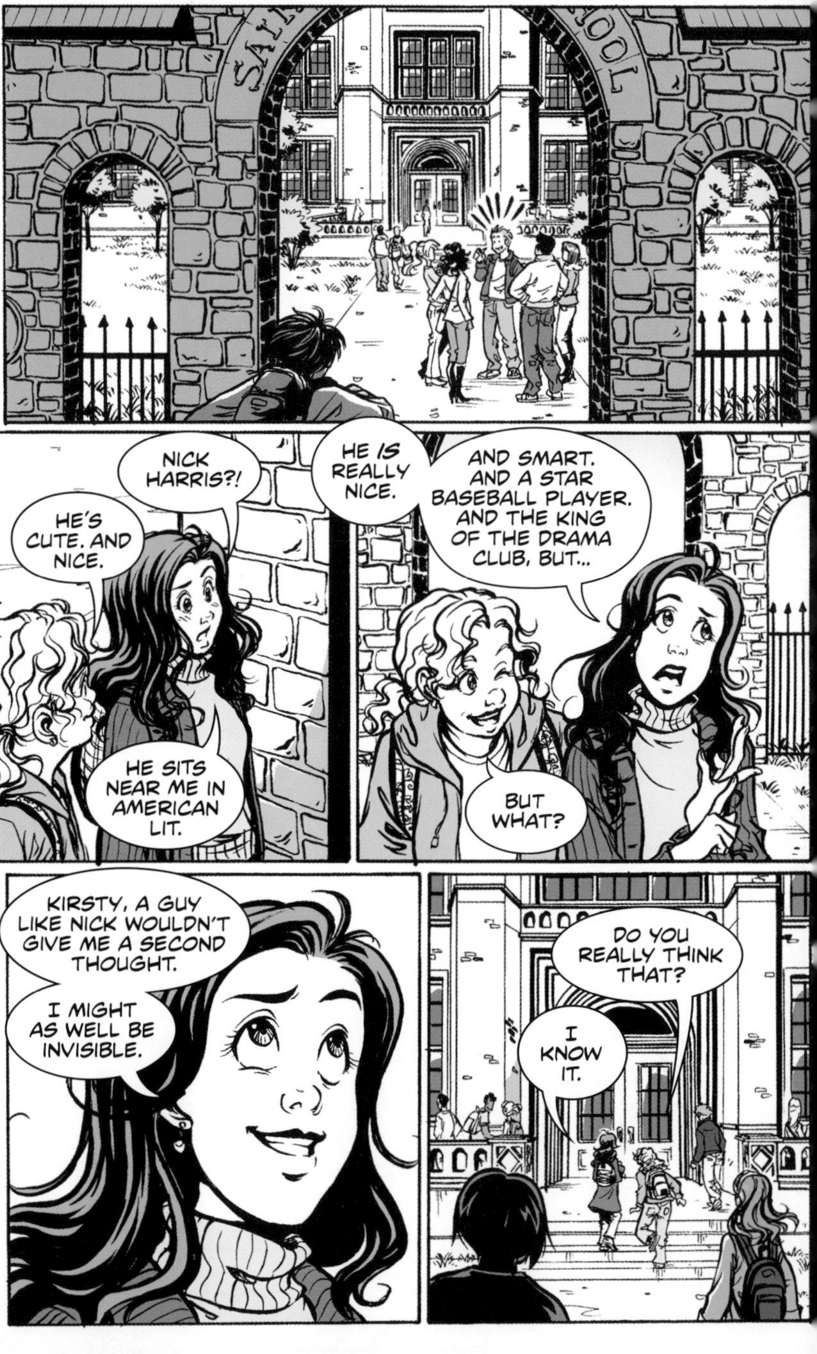

NICK HARRIS?!
HE'S CUTE. AND NICE.
HE SITS NEAR ME IN AMERICAN LIT.
HE *IS* REALLY NICE.
AND SMART. AND A STAR BASEBALL PLAYER. AND THE KING OF THE DRAMA CLUB, BUT...
BUT WHAT?
KIRSTY, A GUY LIKE NICK WOULDN'T GIVE ME A SECOND THOUGHT.
I MIGHT AS WELL BE INVISIBLE.
DO YOU REALLY THINK THAT?
I KNOW IT.

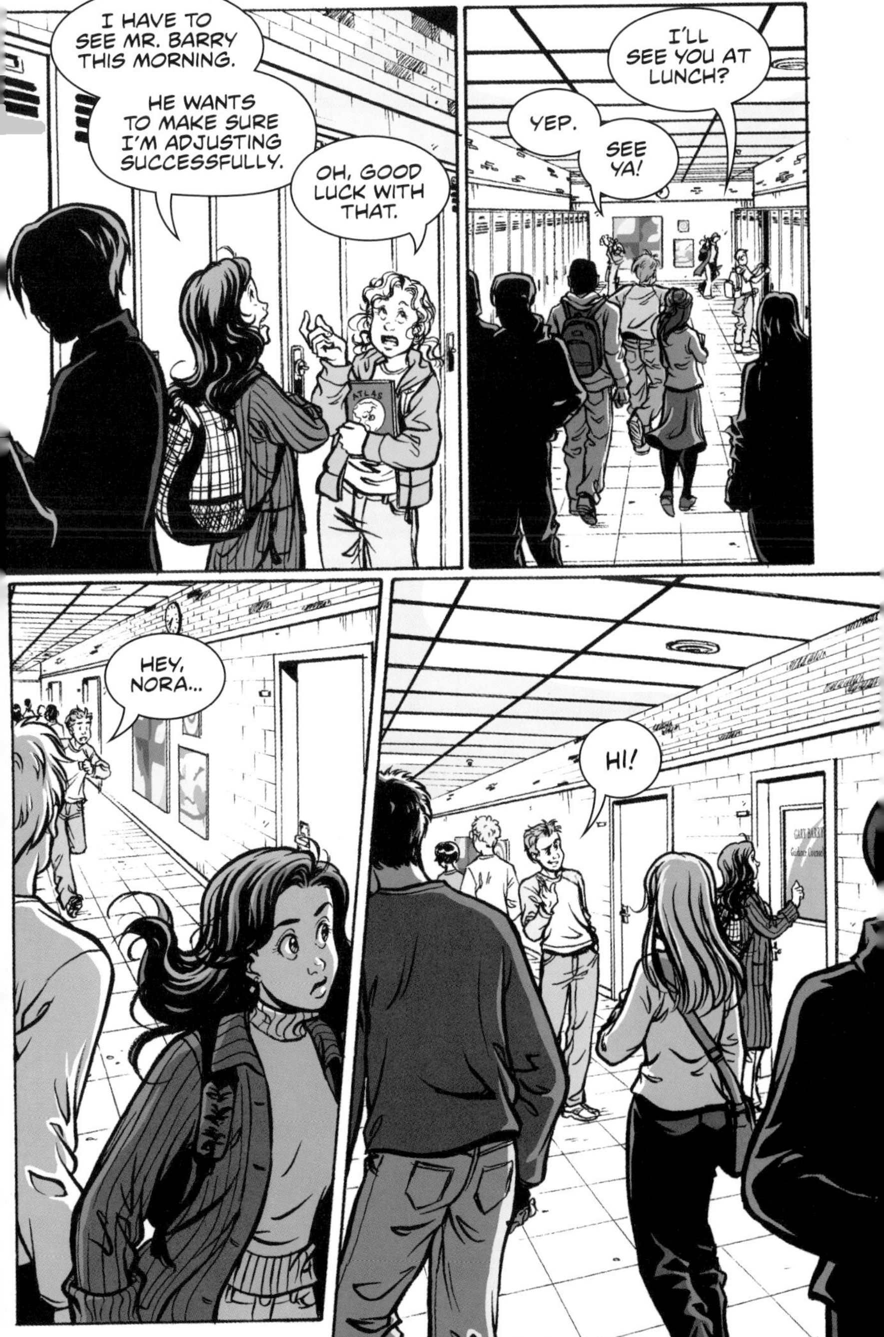
I HAVE TO SEE MR. BARRY THIS MORNING.
HE WANTS TO MAKE SURE I'M ADJUSTING SUCCESSFULLY.
OH, GOOD LUCK WITH THAT.
ATLAS
I'LL SEE YOU AT LUNCH?
YEP.
SEE YA!
HEY, NORA...
HI!

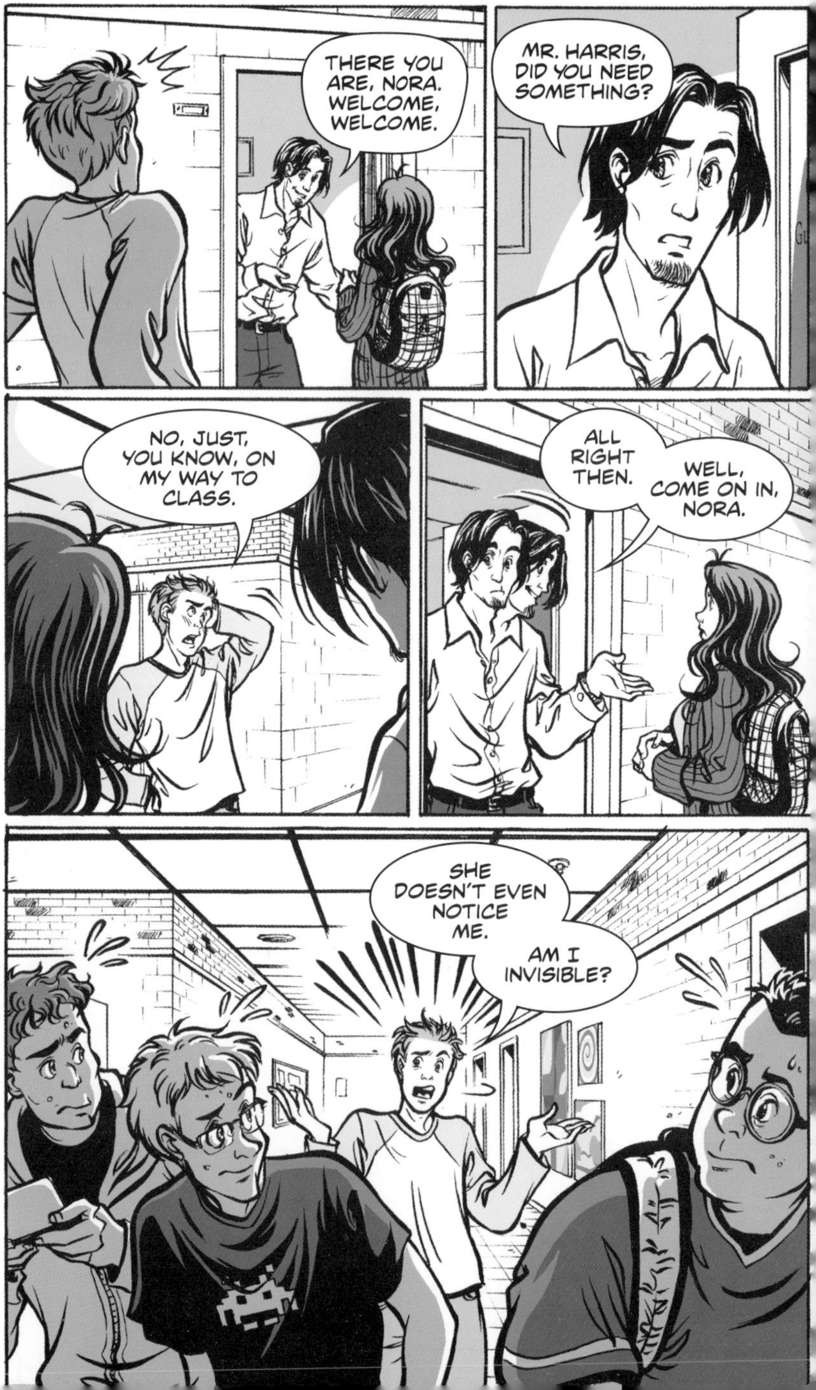
THERE YOU ARE, NORA. WELCOME, WELCOME.
MR. HARRIS, DID YOU NEED SOMETHING?
NO, JUST, YOU KNOW, ON MY WAY TO CLASS.
ALL RIGHT THEN.
WELL, COME ON IN, NORA.
SHE DOESN'T EVEN NOTICE ME.
AM I INVISIBLE?

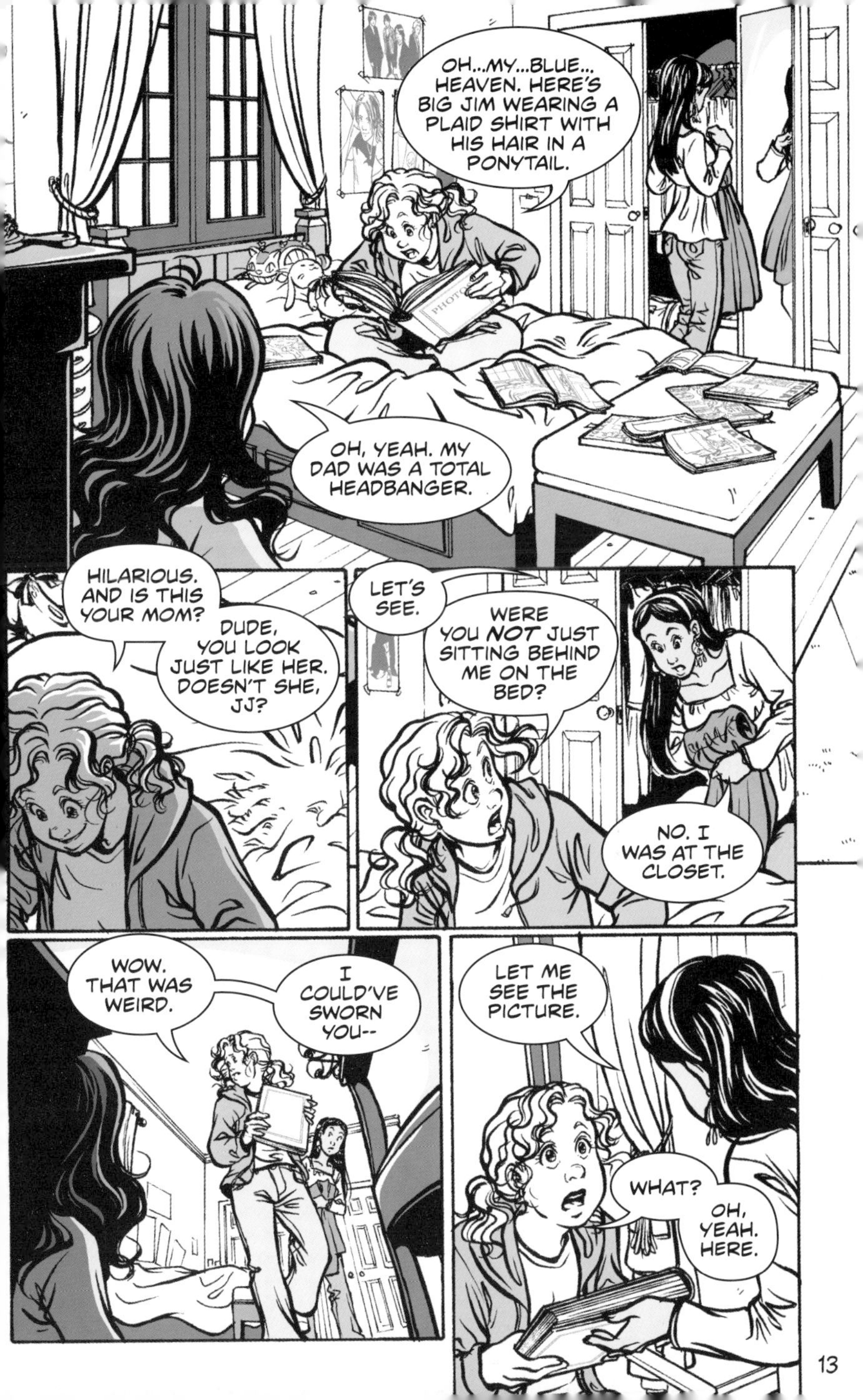
OH...MY...BLUE... HEAVEN. HERE'S BIG JIM WEARING A PLAID SHIRT WITH HIS HAIR IN A PONYTAIL.
OH, YEAH. MY DAD WAS A TOTAL HEADBANGER.
HILARIOUS. AND IS THIS YOUR MOM?
DUDE, YOU LOOK JUST LIKE HER. DOESN'T SHE, JJ?
LET'S SEE.
WERE YOU NOT JUST SITTING BEHIND ME ON THE BED?
NO. I WAS AT THE CLOSET.
WOW. THAT WAS WEIRD.
I COULD'VE SWORN YOU--
LET ME SEE THE PICTURE.
WHAT?
OH, YEAH. HERE.

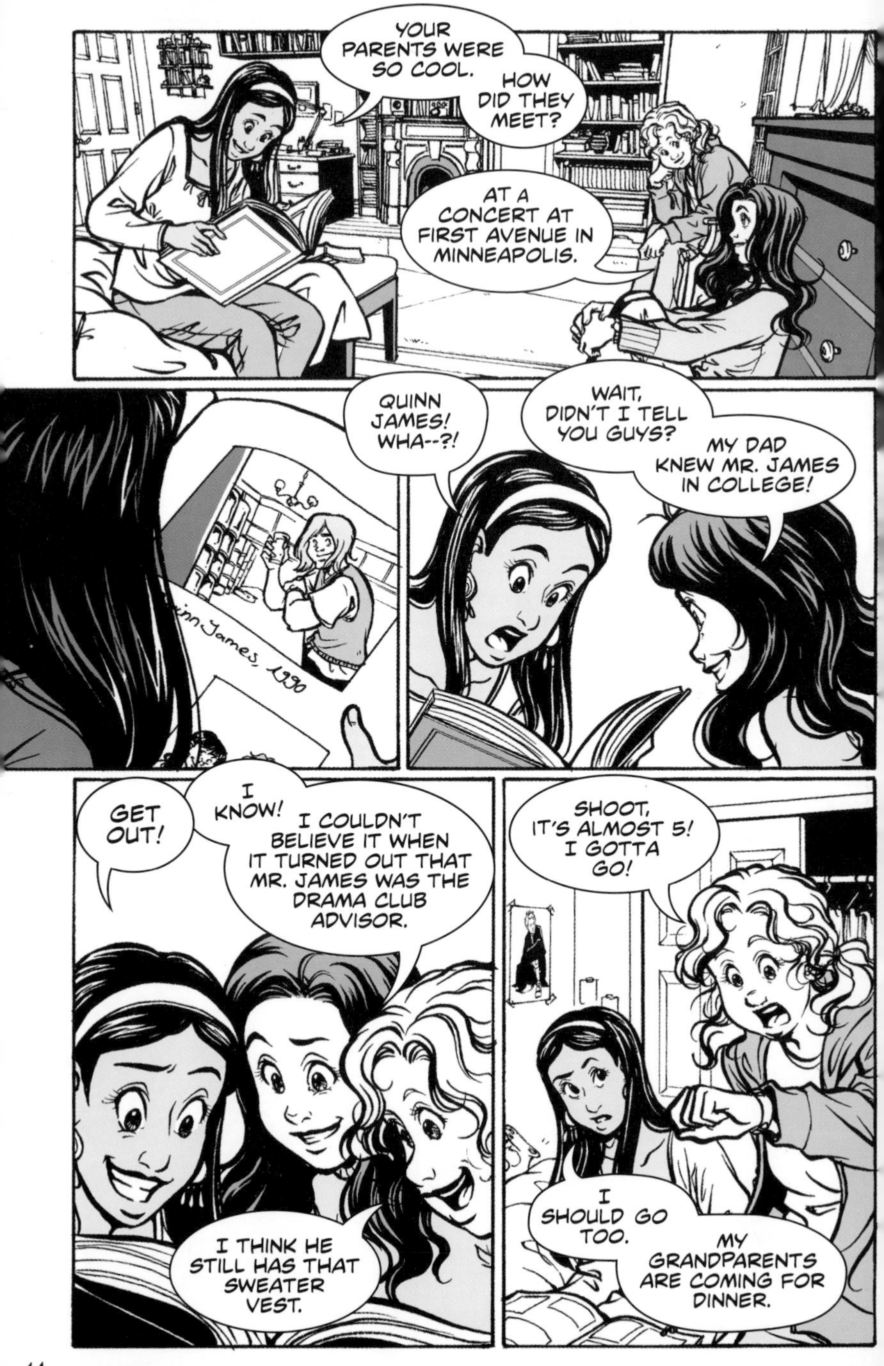
YOUR PARENTS WERE SO COOL.
HOW DID THEY MEET?
AT A CONCERT AT FIRST AVENUE IN MINNEAPOLIS.
QUINN JAMES! WHA--?!
WAIT, DIDN'T I TELL YOU GUYS?
MY DAD KNEW MR. JAMES IN COLLEGE!
GET OUT!
I KNOW!
I COULDN'T BELIEVE IT WHEN IT TURNED OUT THAT MR. JAMES WAS THE DRAMA CLUB ADVISOR.
I THINK HE STILL HAS THAT SWEATER VEST.
SHOOT, IT'S ALMOST 5! I GOTTA GO!
I SHOULD GO TOO.
MY GRANDPARENTS ARE COMING FOR DINNER.

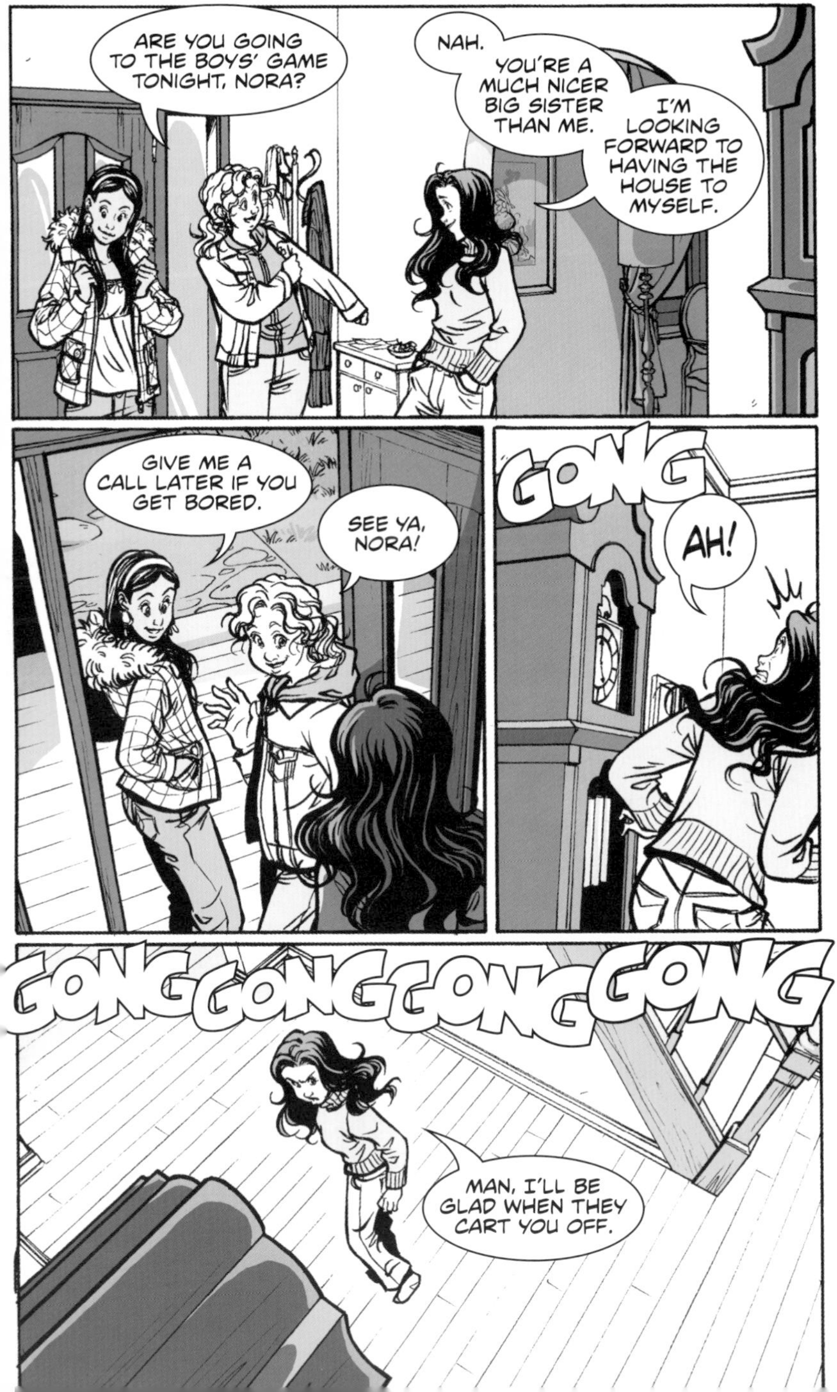
ARE YOU GOING TO THE BOYS' GAME TONIGHT, NORA?
NAH.
YOU'RE A MUCH NICER BIG SISTER THAN ME.
I'M LOOKING FORWARD TO HAVING THE HOUSE TO MYSELF.
GIVE ME A CALL LATER IF YOU GET BORED.
SEE YA, NORA!
GONG
AH!
GONG GONG GONG GONG
MAN, I'LL BE GLAD WHEN THEY CART YOU OFF.

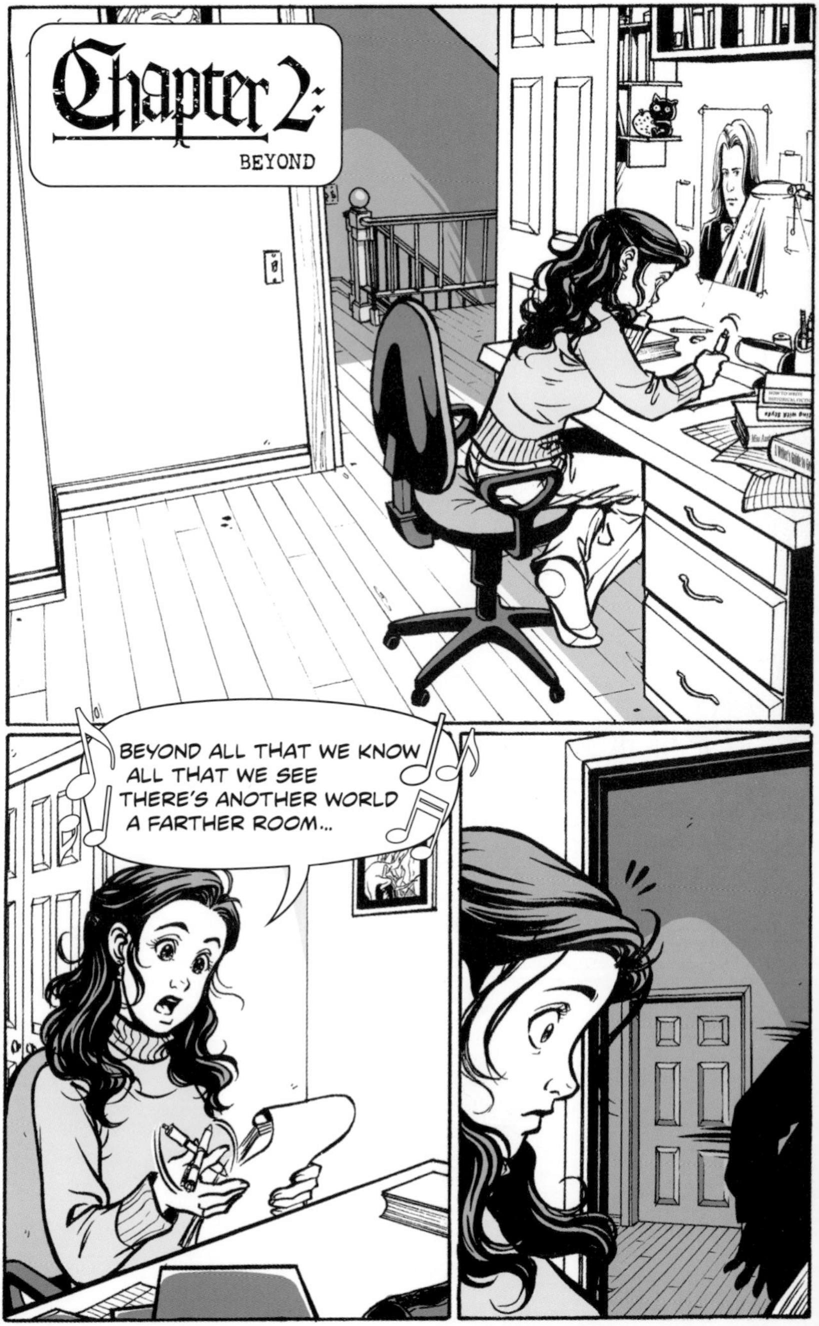
Chapter 2:
BEYOND
BEYOND ALL THAT WE KNOW ALL THAT WE SEE THERE'S ANOTHER WORLD A FARTHER ROOM...

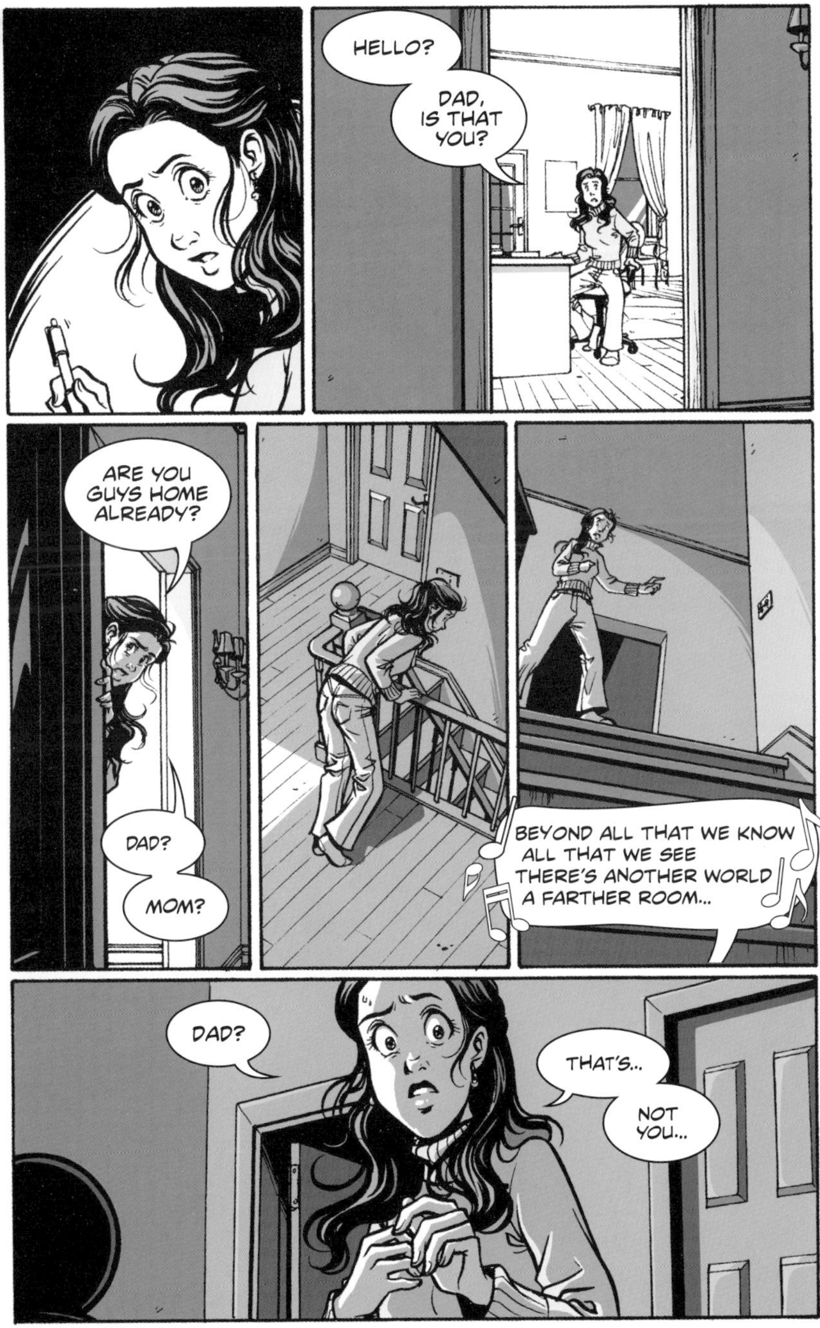
HELLO?
DAD, IS THAT YOU?
ARE YOU GUYS HOME ALREADY?
DAD?
MOM?
BEYOND ALL THAT WE KNOW ALL THAT WE SEE THERE'S ANOTHER WORLD A FARTHER ROOM...
DAD?
THAT'S...
NOT YOU...

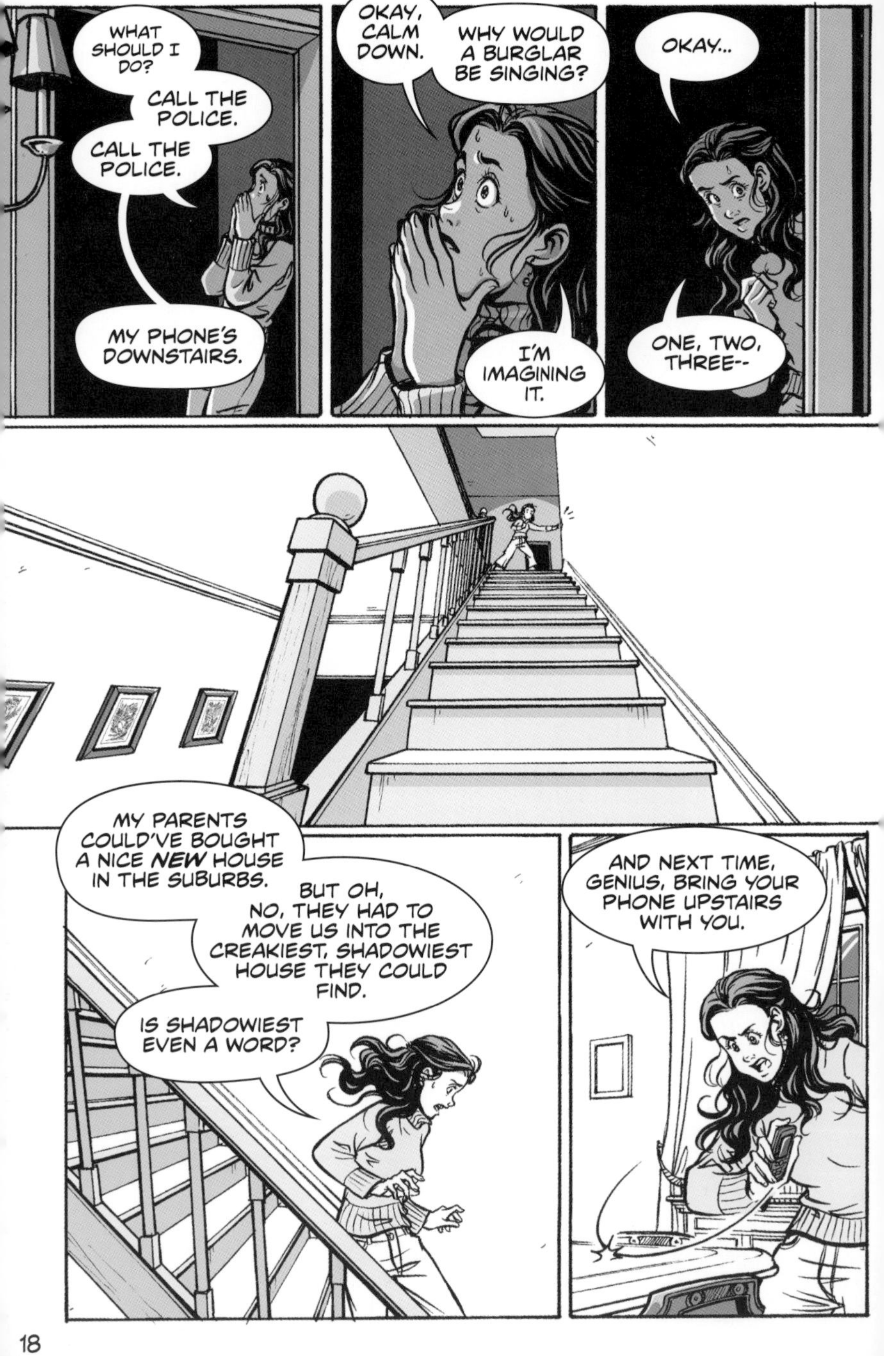
WHAT SHOULD I DO?
CALL THE POLICE.
CALL THE POLICE.
MY PHONE'S DOWNSTAIRS.
OKAY, CALM DOWN.
WHY WOULD A BURGLAR BE SINGING?
I'M IMAGINING IT.
OKAY...
ONE, TWO, THREE--
MY PARENTS COULD'VE BOUGHT A NICE *NEW* HOUSE IN THE SUBURBS.
BUT OH, NO, THEY HAD TO MOVE US INTO THE CREAKIEST, SHADOWIEST HOUSE THEY COULD FIND.
IS SHADOWIEST EVEN A WORD?
AND NEXT TIME, GENIUS, BRING YOUR PHONE UPSTAIRS WITH YOU.

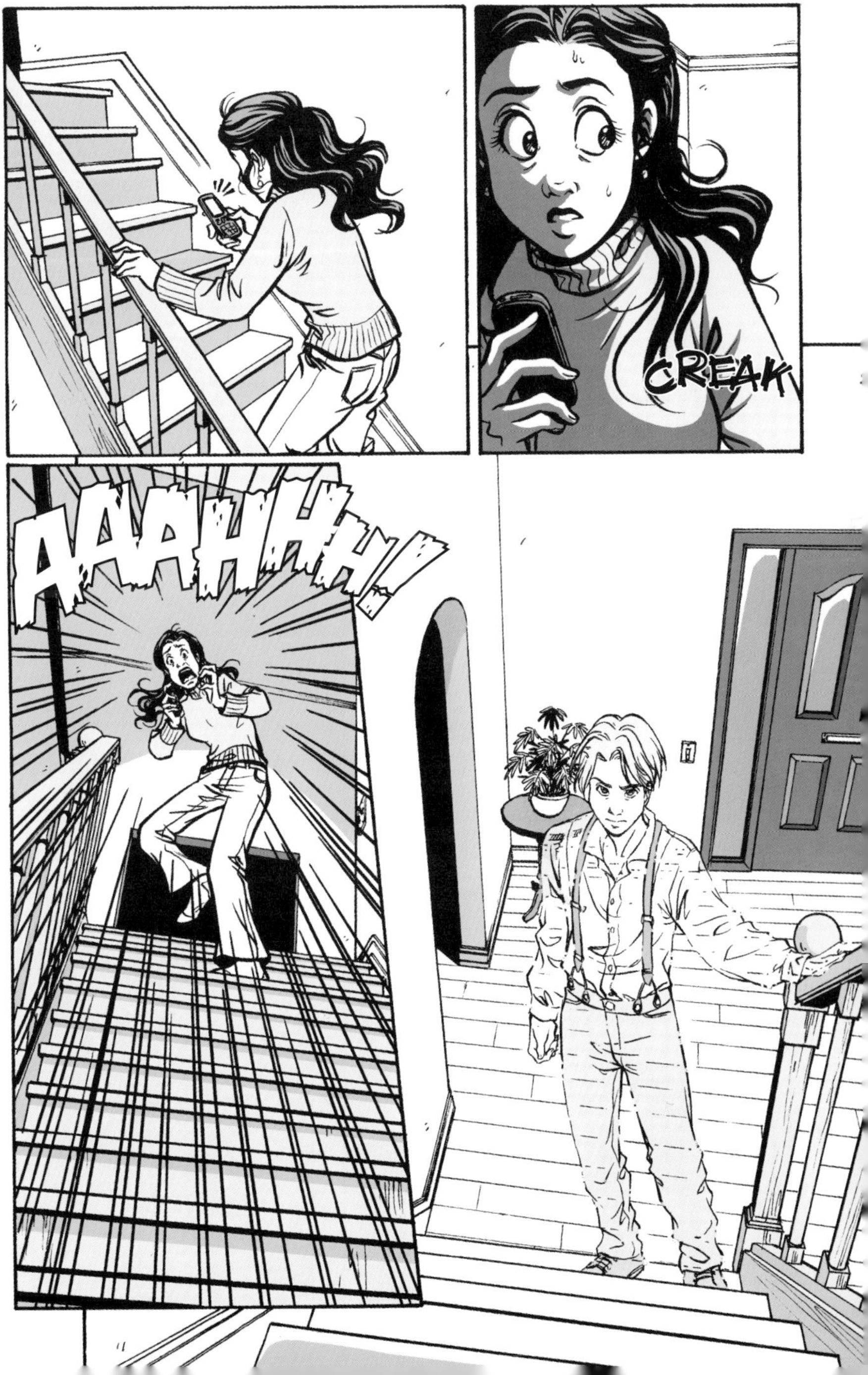
CREAK
AAAHHH!

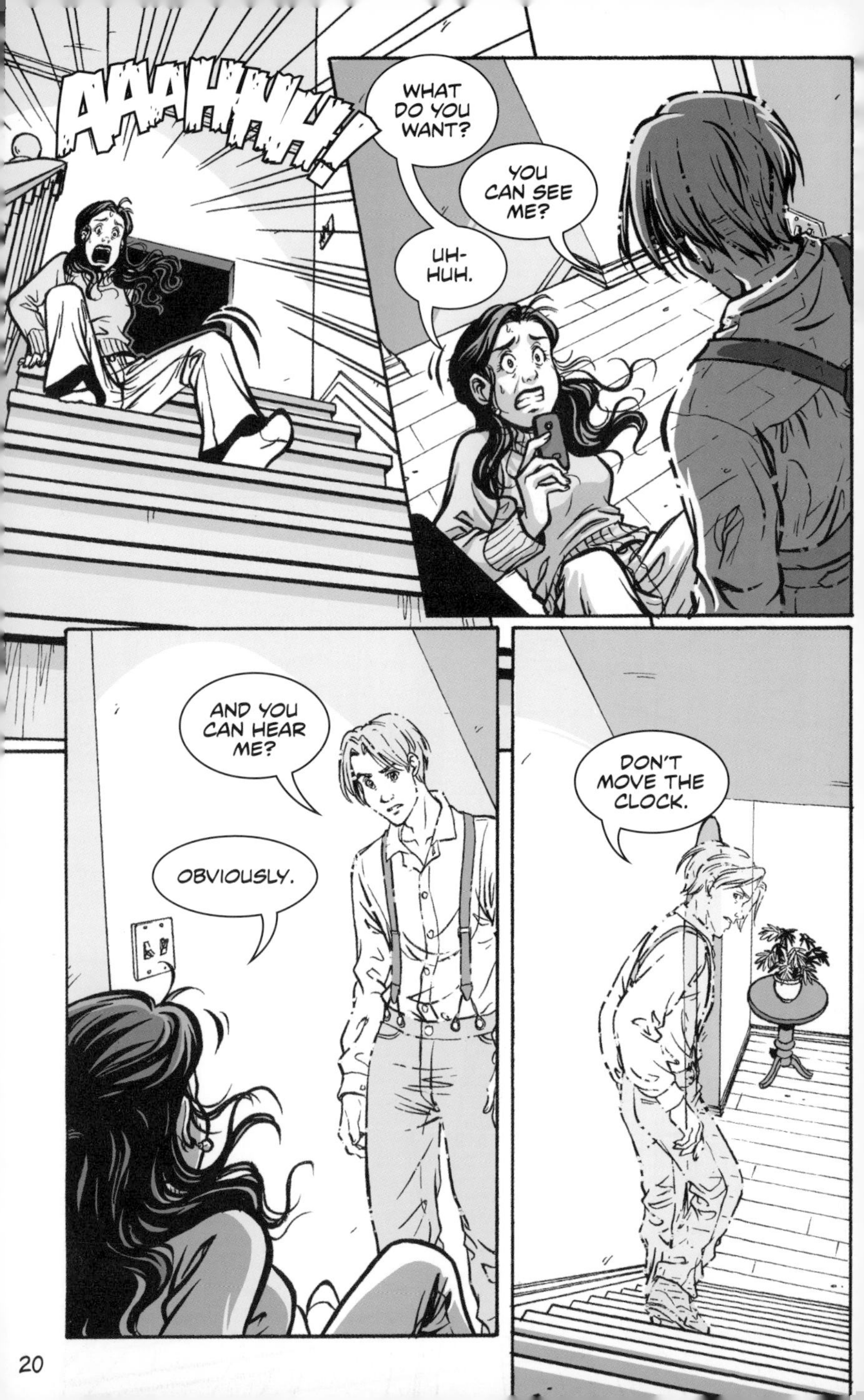
AAAHHHH!!
WHAT DO YOU WANT?
YOU CAN SEE ME?
UH-HUH.
AND YOU CAN HEAR ME?
OBVIOUSLY.
DON'T MOVE THE CLOCK.

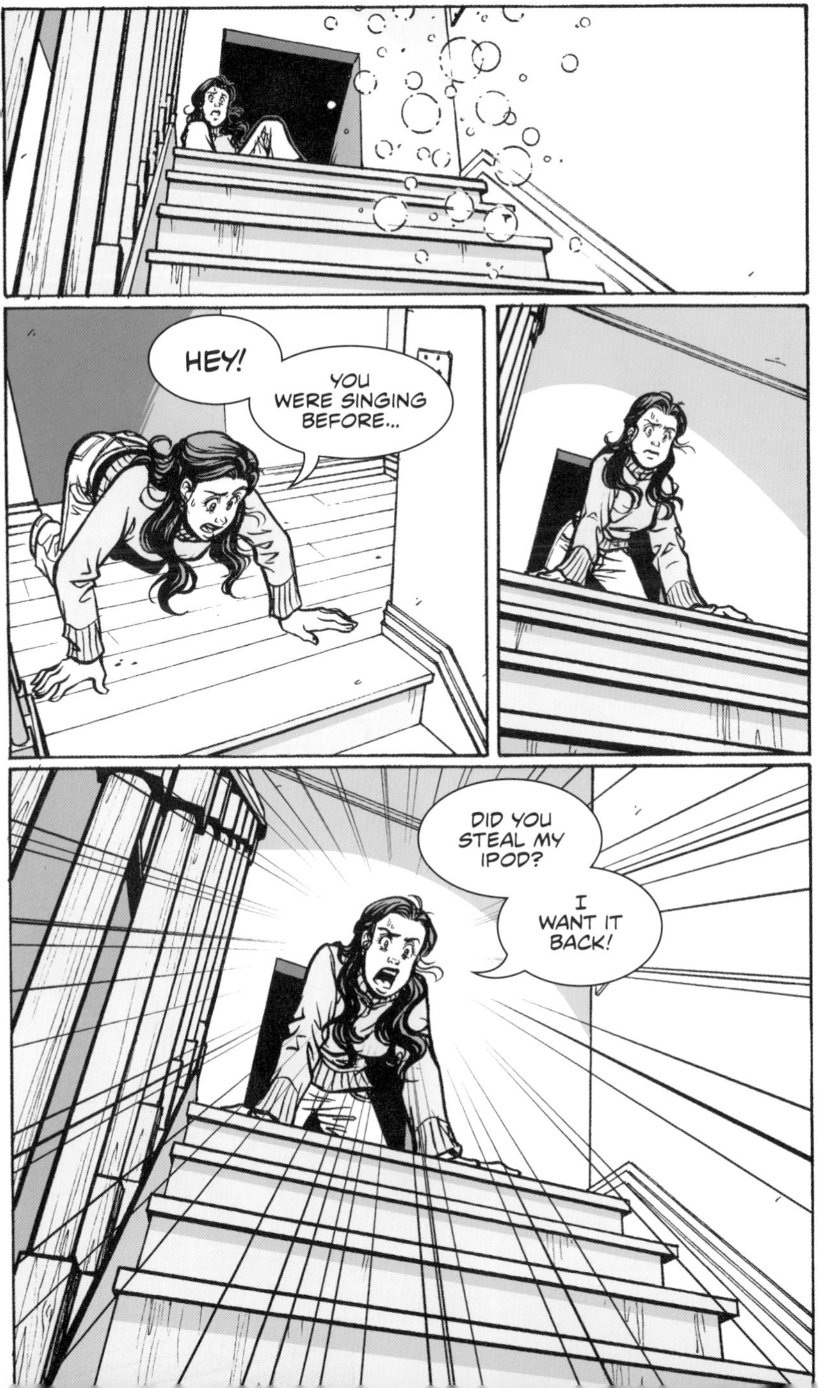
HEY!
YOU WERE SINGING BEFORE...
DID YOU STEAL MY IPOD?
I WANT IT BACK!

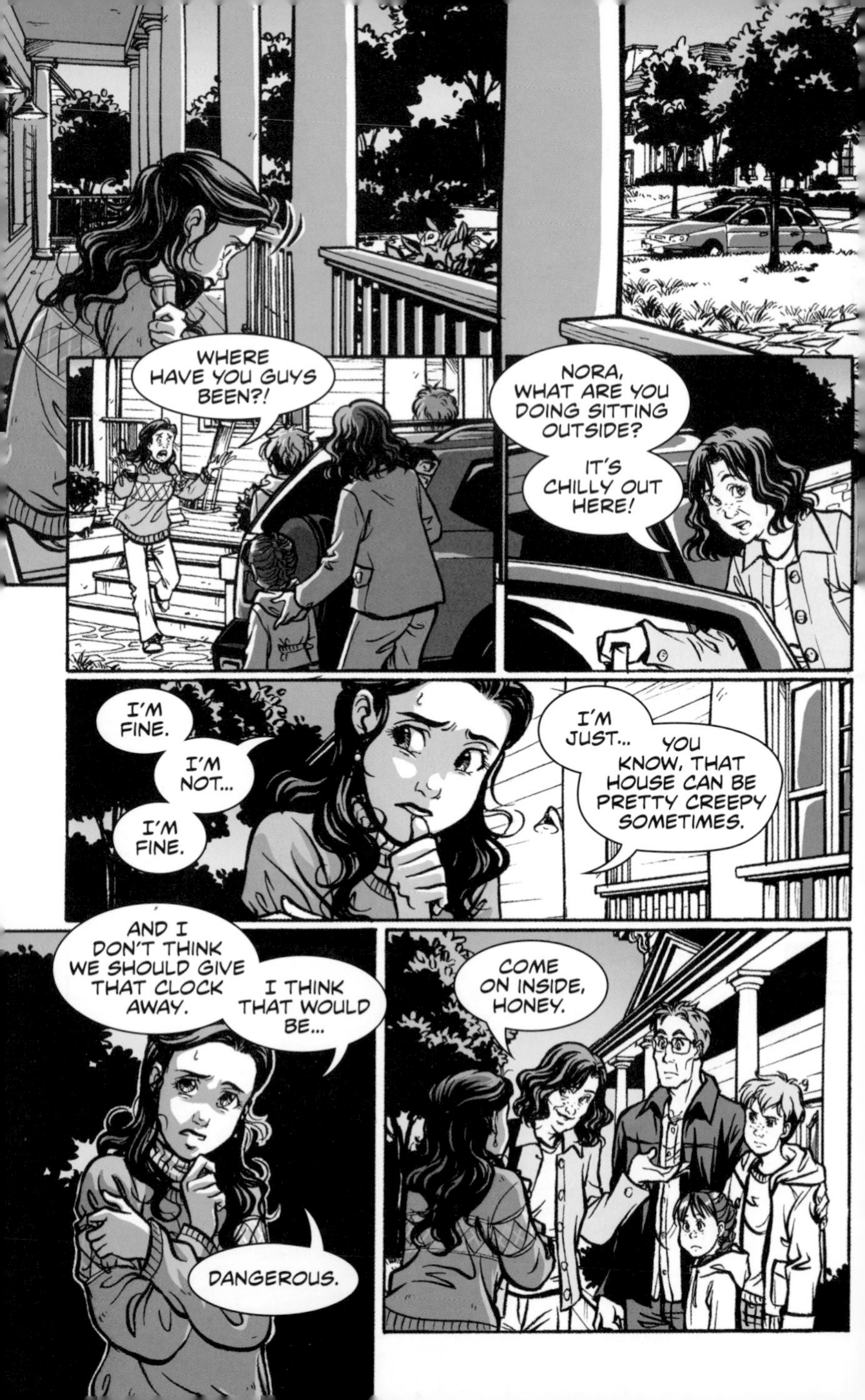
WHERE HAVE YOU GUYS BEEN?!
NORA, WHAT ARE YOU DOING SITTING OUTSIDE?
IT'S CHILLY OUT HERE!
I'M FINE.
I'M NOT...
I'M FINE.
I'M JUST... YOU KNOW, THAT HOUSE CAN BE PRETTY CREEPY SOMETIMES.
AND I DON'T THINK WE SHOULD GIVE THAT CLOCK AWAY.
I THINK THAT WOULD BE...
DANGEROUS.
COME ON INSIDE, HONEY.

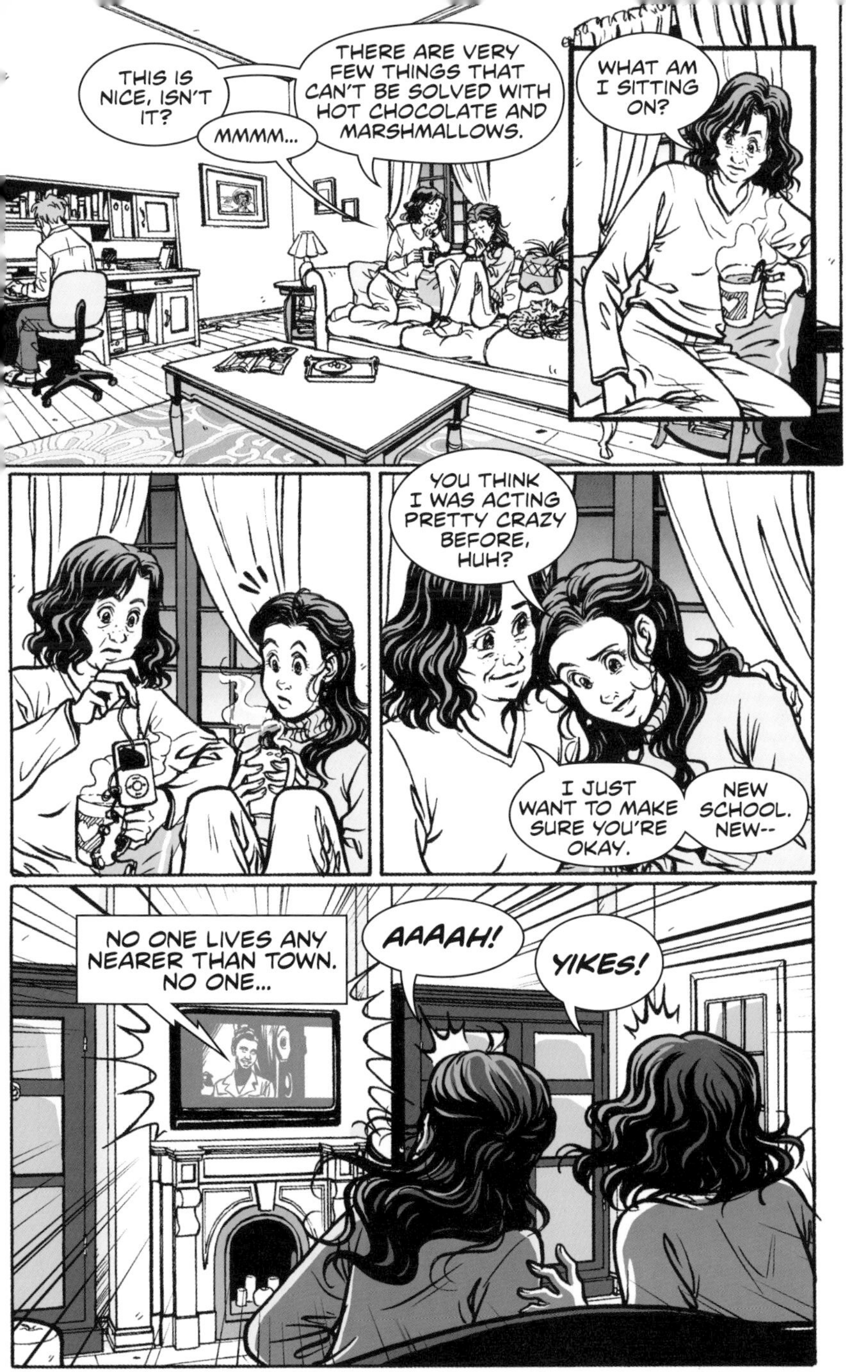
THIS IS NICE, ISN'T IT?
MMMM...
THERE ARE VERY FEW THINGS THAT CAN'T BE SOLVED WITH HOT CHOCOLATE AND MARSHMALLOWS.
WHAT AM I SITTING ON?
YOU THINK I WAS ACTING PRETTY CRAZY BEFORE, HUH?
I JUST WANT TO MAKE SURE YOU'RE OKAY.
NEW SCHOOL. NEW--
NO ONE LIVES ANY NEARER THAN TOWN. NO ONE...
AAAAH!
YIKES!

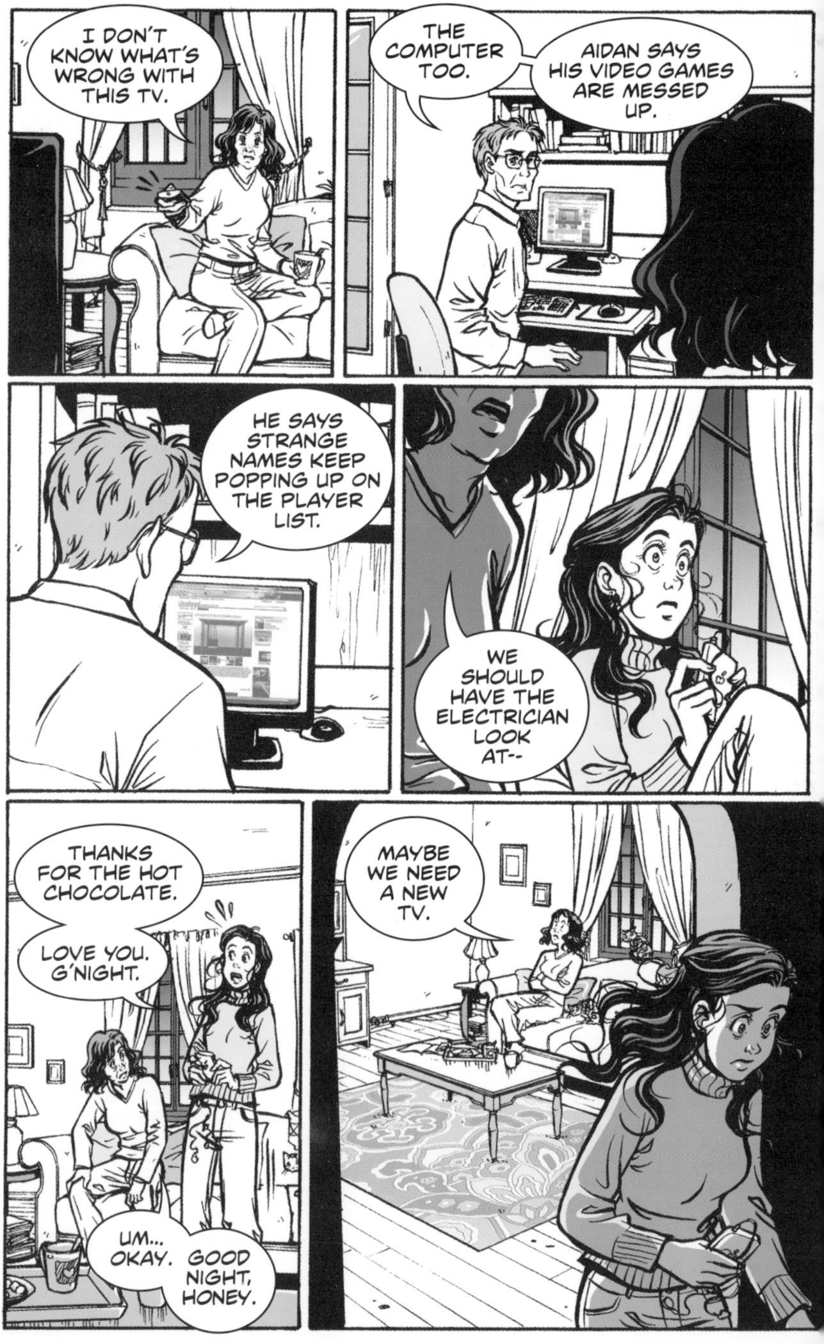
I DON'T KNOW WHAT'S WRONG WITH THIS TV.
THE COMPUTER TOO.
AIDAN SAYS HIS VIDEO GAMES ARE MESSED UP.
HE SAYS STRANGE NAMES KEEP POPPING UP ON THE PLAYER LIST.
WE SHOULD HAVE THE ELECTRICIAN LOOK AT--
THANKS FOR THE HOT CHOCOLATE.
LOVE YOU. G'NIGHT.
UM... OKAY.
GOOD NIGHT, HONEY.
MAYBE WE NEED A NEW TV.

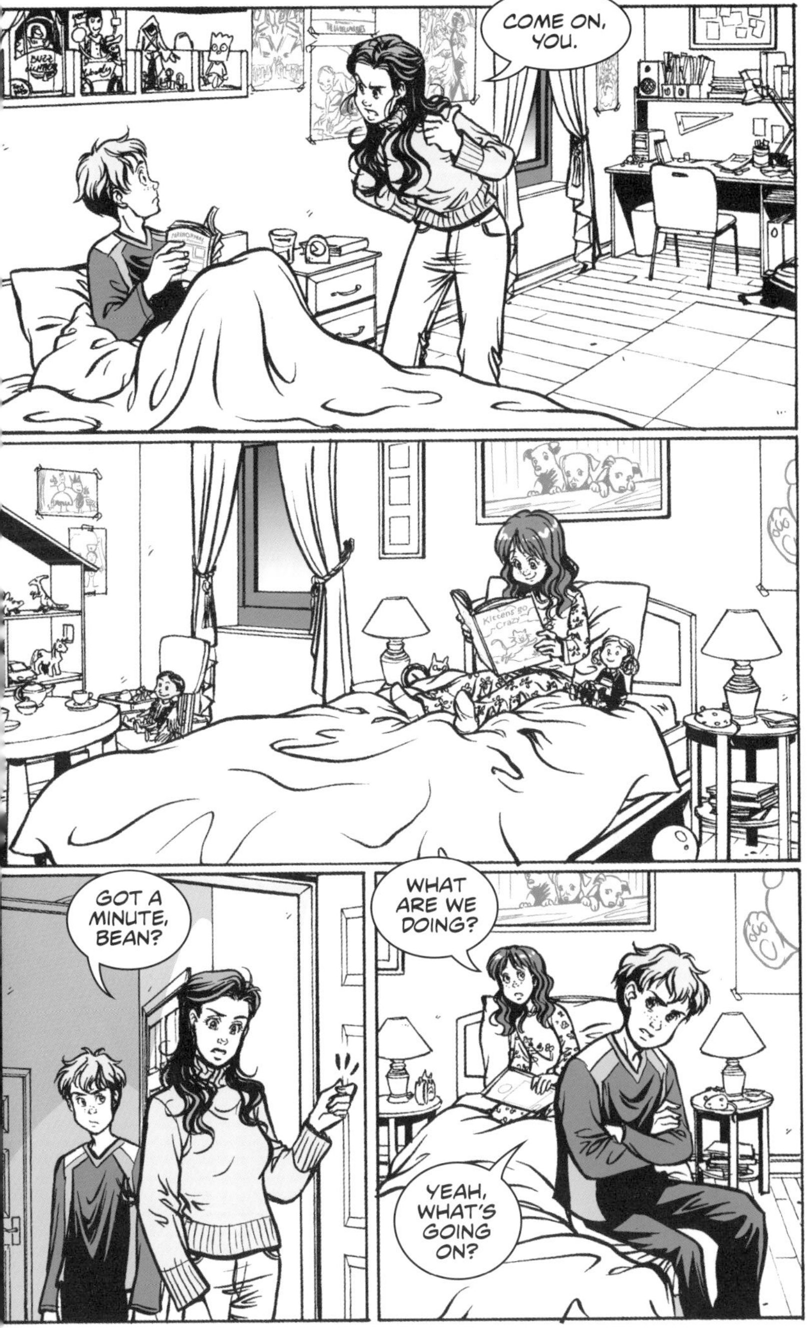
COME ON, YOU.
Kittens go Crazy
GOT A MINUTE, BEAN?
WHAT ARE WE DOING?
YEAH, WHAT'S GOING ON?

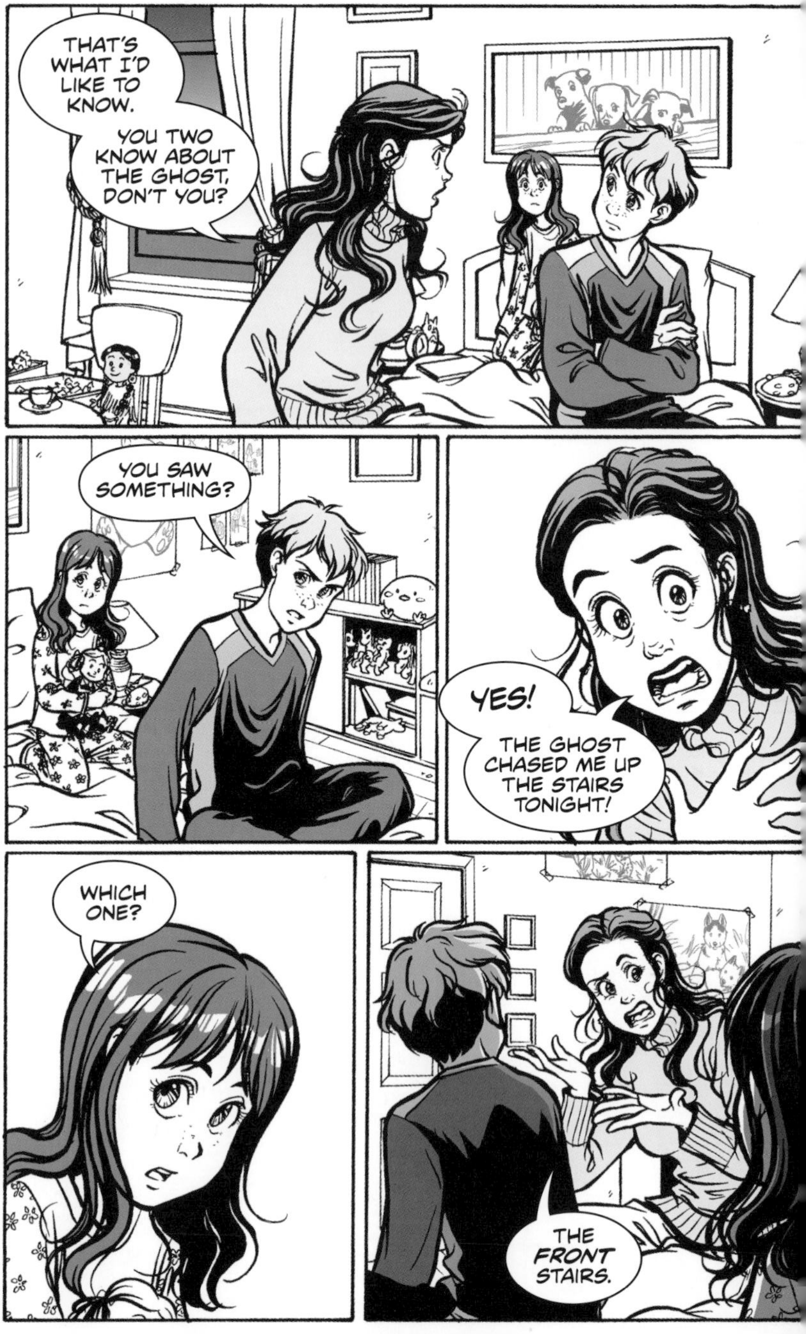
THAT'S WHAT I'D LIKE TO KNOW.
YOU TWO KNOW ABOUT THE GHOST, DON'T YOU?
YOU SAW SOMETHING?
YES!
THE GHOST CHASED ME UP THE STAIRS TONIGHT!
WHICH ONE?
THE FRONT STAIRS.

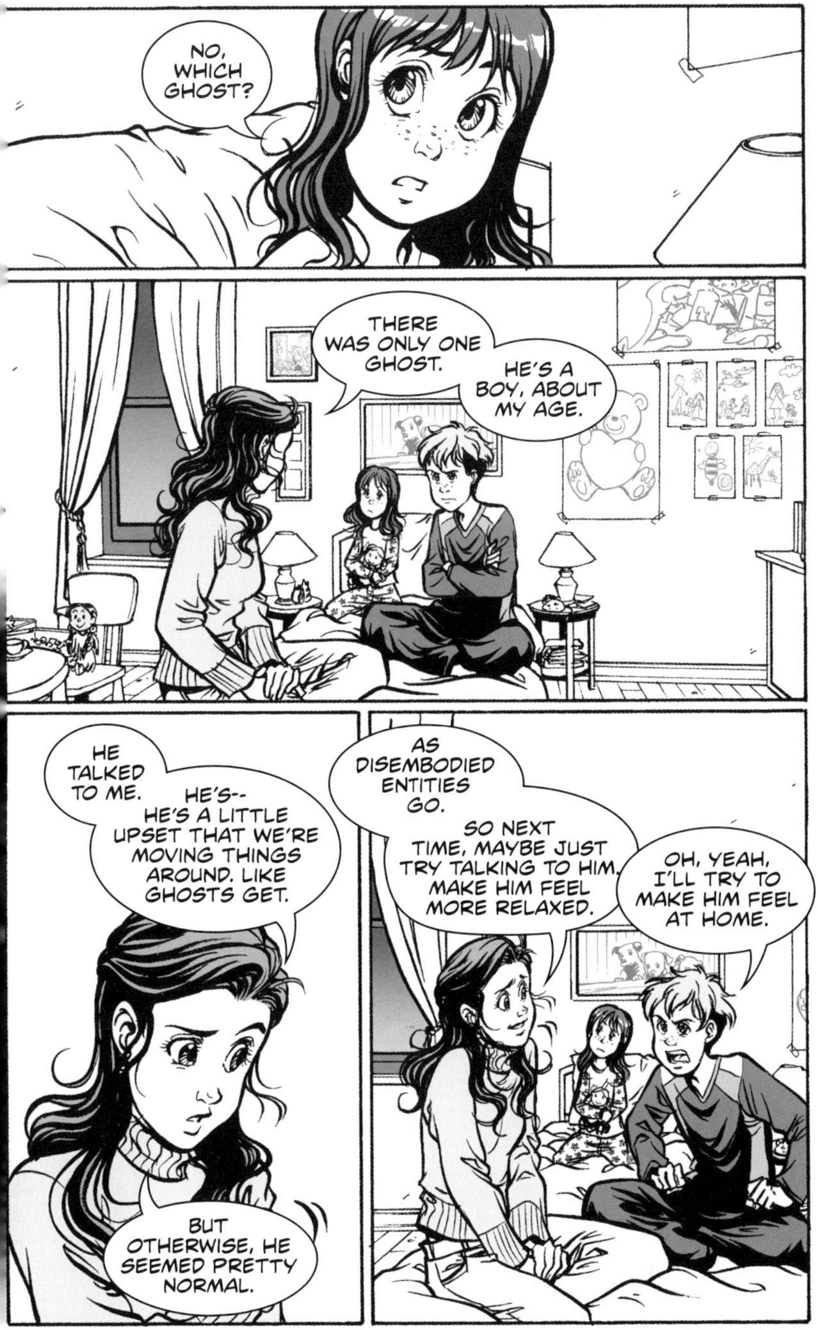
NO, WHICH GHOST?
THERE WAS ONLY ONE GHOST.
HE'S A BOY, ABOUT MY AGE.
HE TALKED TO ME.
HE'S-- HE'S A LITTLE UPSET THAT WE'RE MOVING THINGS AROUND. LIKE GHOSTS GET.
BUT OTHERWISE, HE SEEMED PRETTY NORMAL.
AS DISEMBODIED ENTITIES GO.
SO NEXT TIME, MAYBE JUST TRY TALKING TO HIM. MAKE HIM FEEL MORE RELAXED.
OH, YEAH, I'LL TRY TO MAKE HIM FEEL AT HOME.

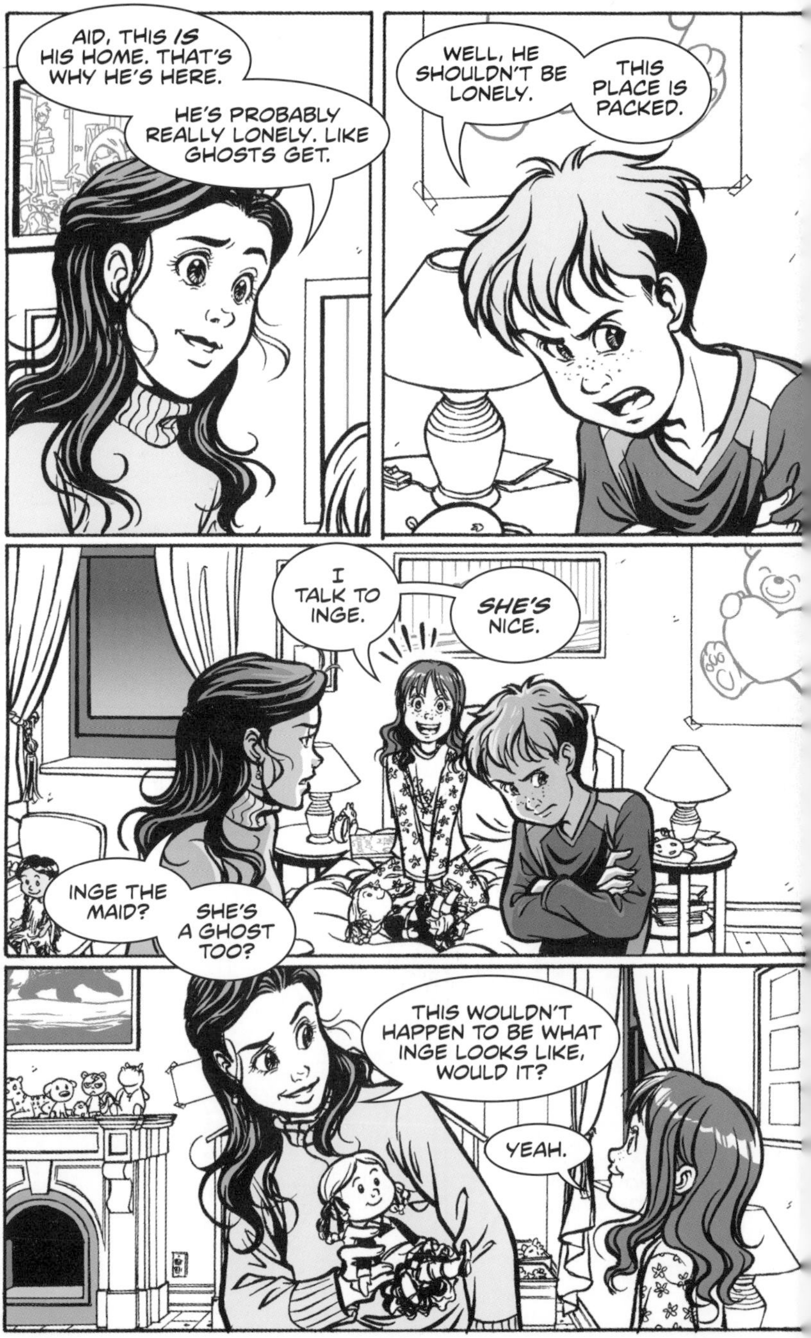
AID, THIS *IS* HIS HOME. THAT'S WHY HE'S HERE.
HE'S PROBABLY REALLY LONELY. LIKE GHOSTS GET.
WELL, HE SHOULDN'T BE LONELY.
THIS PLACE IS PACKED.
I TALK TO INGE.
SHE'S NICE.
INGE THE MAID?
SHE'S A GHOST TOO?
THIS WOULDN'T HAPPEN TO BE WHAT INGE LOOKS LIKE, WOULD IT?
YEAH.

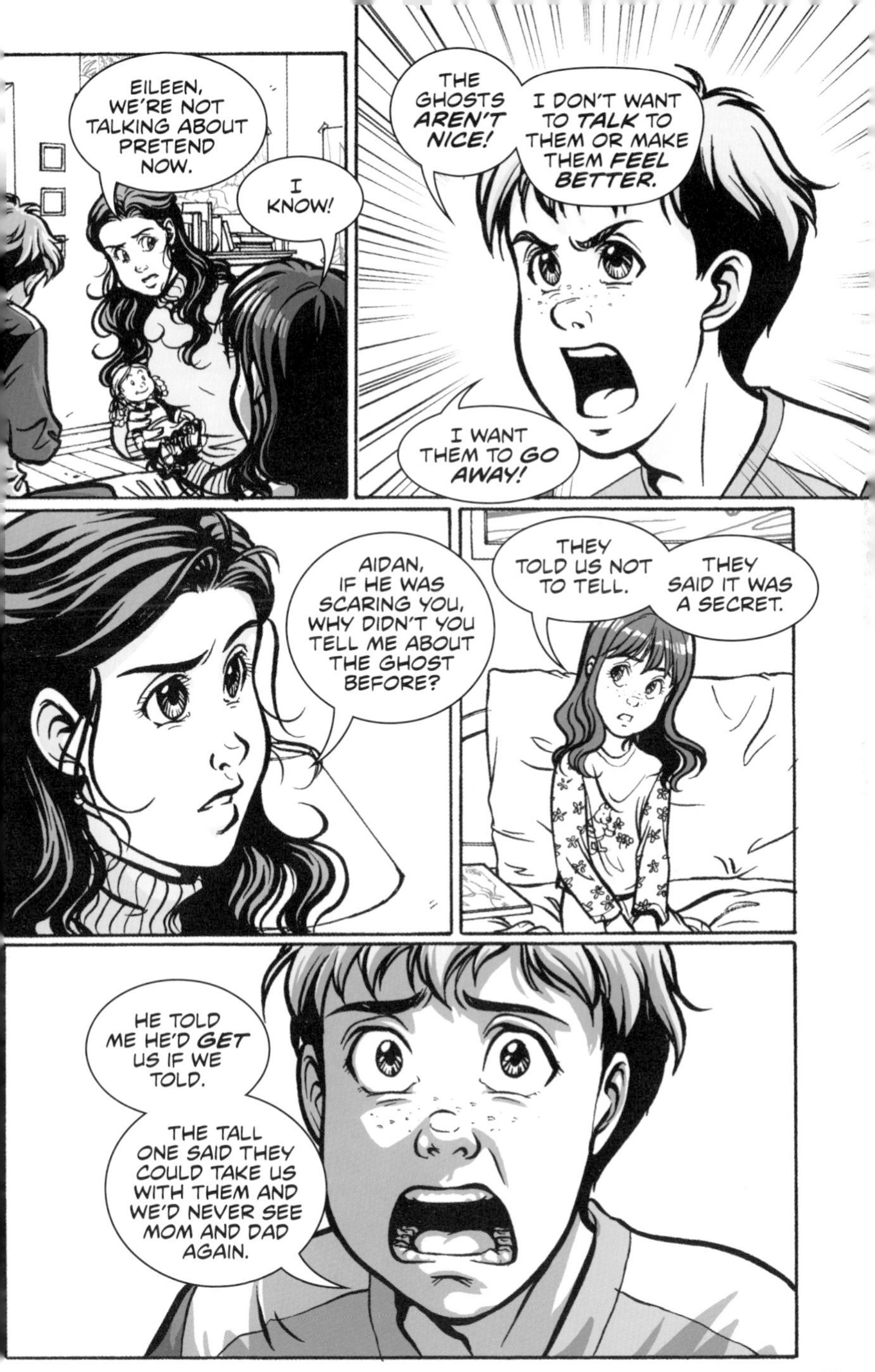
EILEEN, WE'RE NOT TALKING ABOUT PRETEND NOW.
I KNOW!
THE GHOSTS *AREN'T NICE!*
I DON'T WANT TO *TALK* TO THEM OR MAKE THEM *FEEL BETTER.*
I WANT THEM TO *GO AWAY!*
AIDAN, IF HE WAS SCARING YOU, WHY DIDN'T YOU TELL ME ABOUT THE GHOST BEFORE?
THEY TOLD US NOT TO TELL.
THEY SAID IT WAS A SECRET.
HE TOLD ME HE'D *GET* US IF WE TOLD.
THE TALL ONE SAID THEY COULD TAKE US WITH THEM AND WE'D NEVER SEE MOM AND DAD AGAIN.

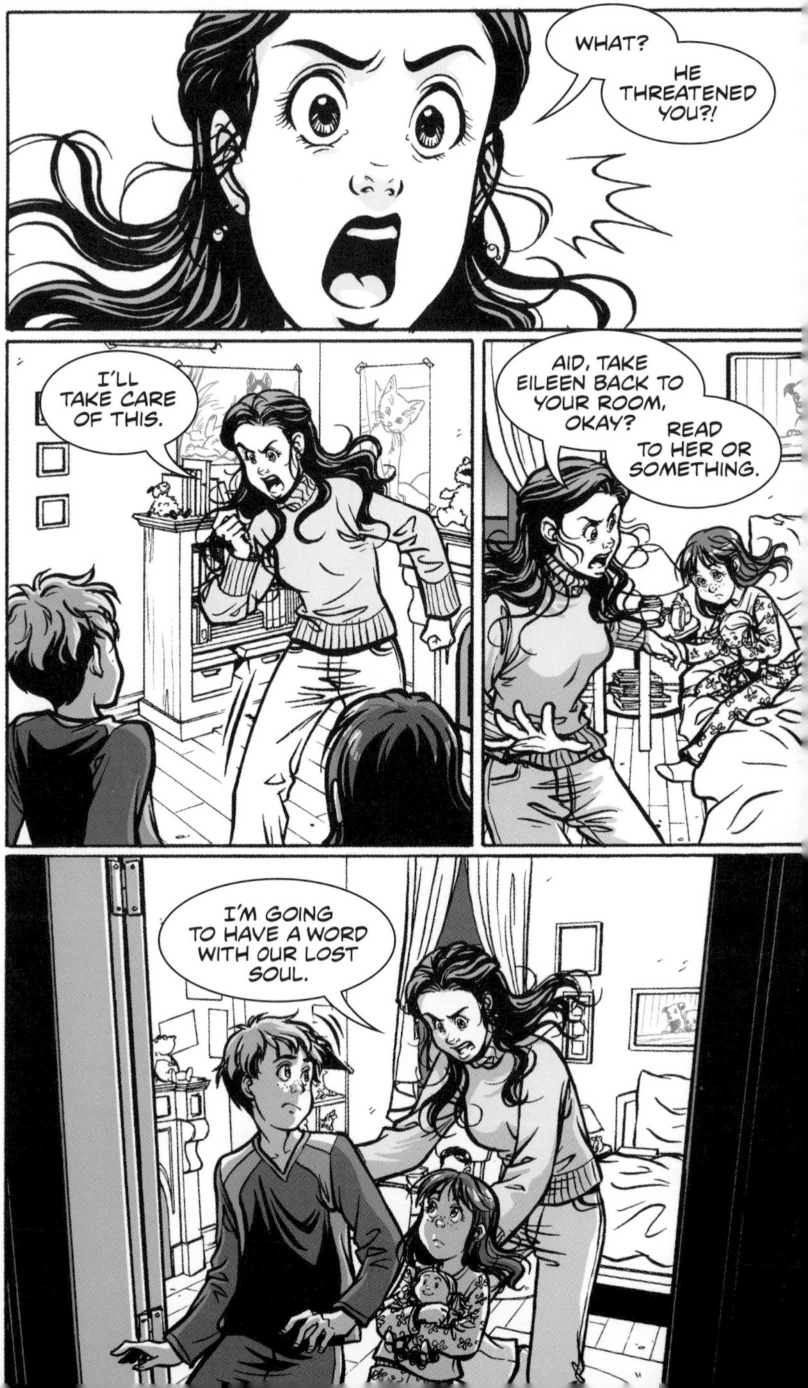
WHAT?
HE THREATENED YOU?!
I'LL TAKE CARE OF THIS.
AID, TAKE EILEEN BACK TO YOUR ROOM, OKAY?
READ TO HER OR SOMETHING.
I'M GOING TO HAVE A WORD WITH OUR LOST SOUL.

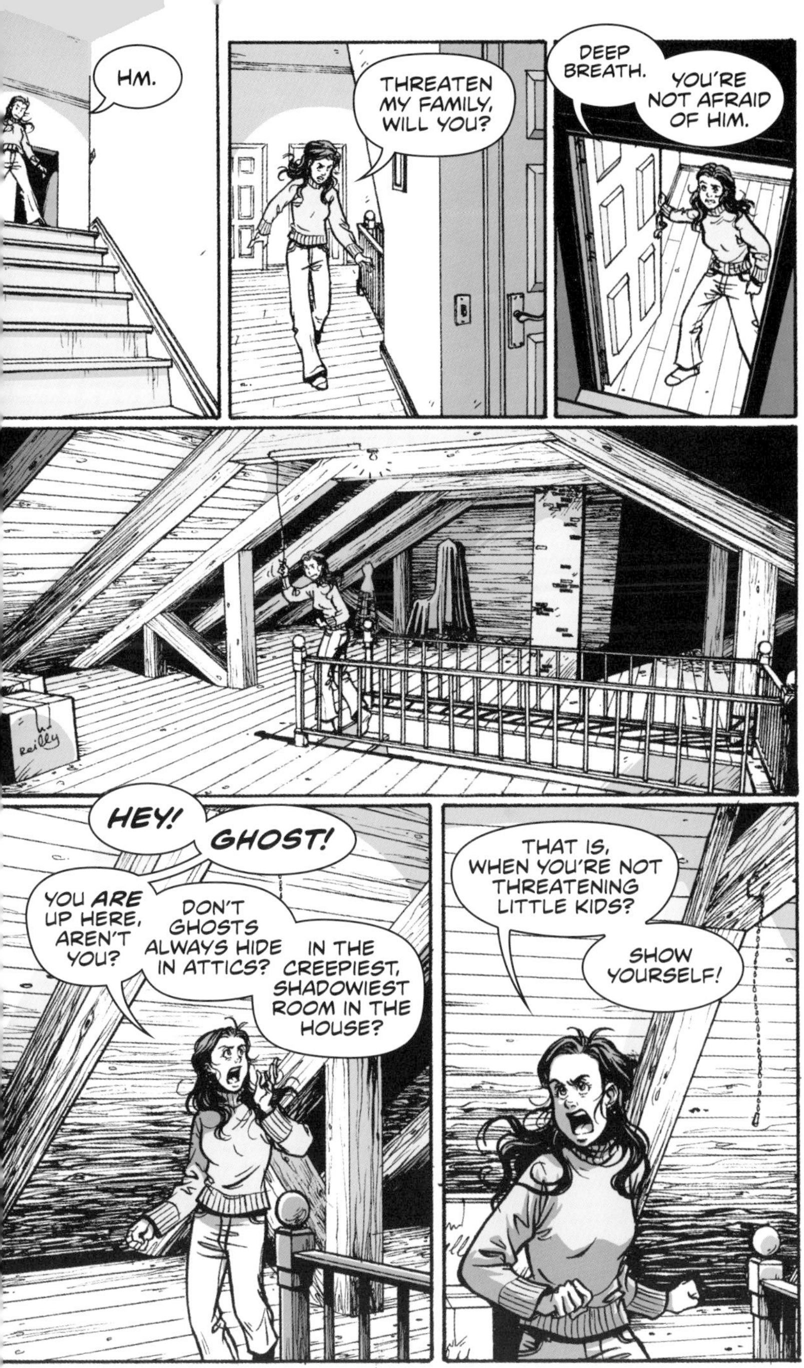
HM.
THREATEN MY FAMILY, WILL YOU?
DEEP BREATH.
YOU'RE NOT AFRAID OF HIM.
Reilly
HEY!
GHOST!
YOU ARE UP HERE, AREN'T YOU?
DON'T GHOSTS ALWAYS HIDE IN ATTICS?
IN THE CREEPIEST, SHADOWIEST ROOM IN THE HOUSE?
THAT IS, WHEN YOU'RE NOT THREATENING LITTLE KIDS?
SHOW YOURSELF!

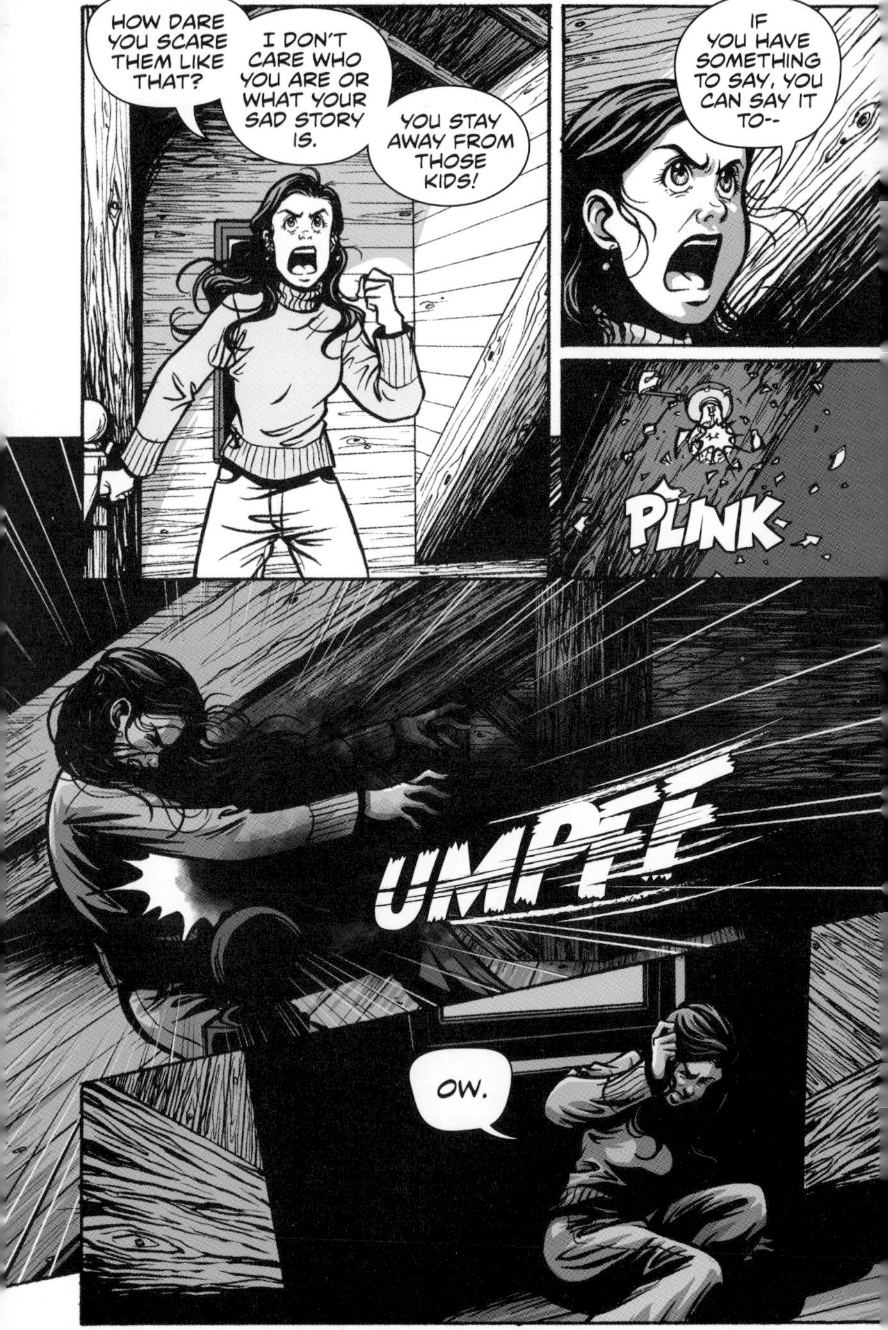
HOW DARE YOU SCARE THEM LIKE THAT?
I DON'T CARE WHO YOU ARE OR WHAT YOUR SAD STORY IS.
YOU STAY AWAY FROM THOSE KIDS!
IF YOU HAVE SOMETHING TO SAY, YOU CAN SAY IT TO--
PLINK
UMPF!
OW.

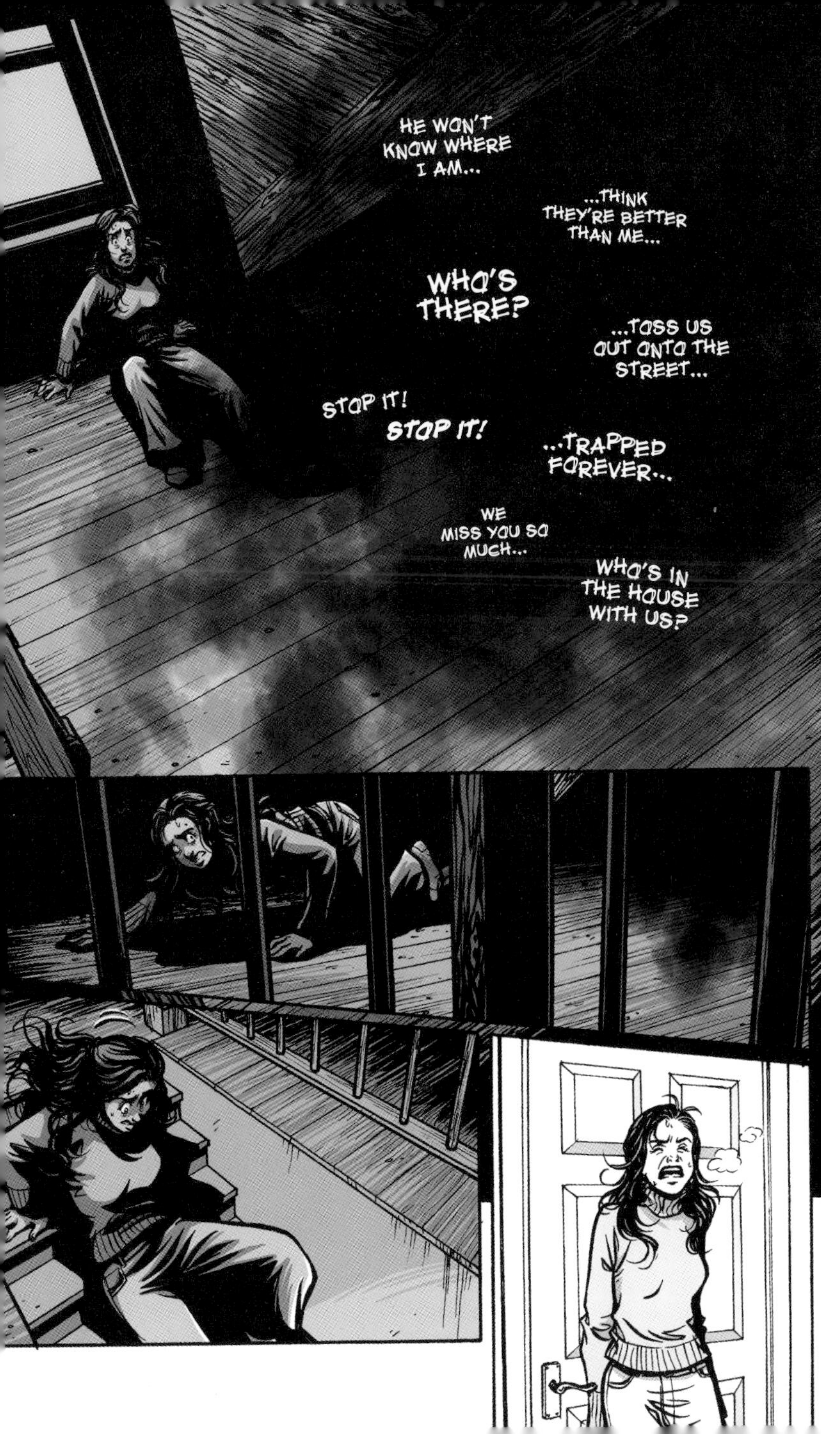
HE WON'T KNOW WHERE I AM...
...THINK THEY'RE BETTER THAN ME...
WHO'S THERE?
...TOSS US OUT ONTO THE STREET...
STOP IT!
STOP IT!
...TRAPPED FOREVER...
WE MISS YOU SO MUCH...
WHO'S IN THE HOUSE WITH US?

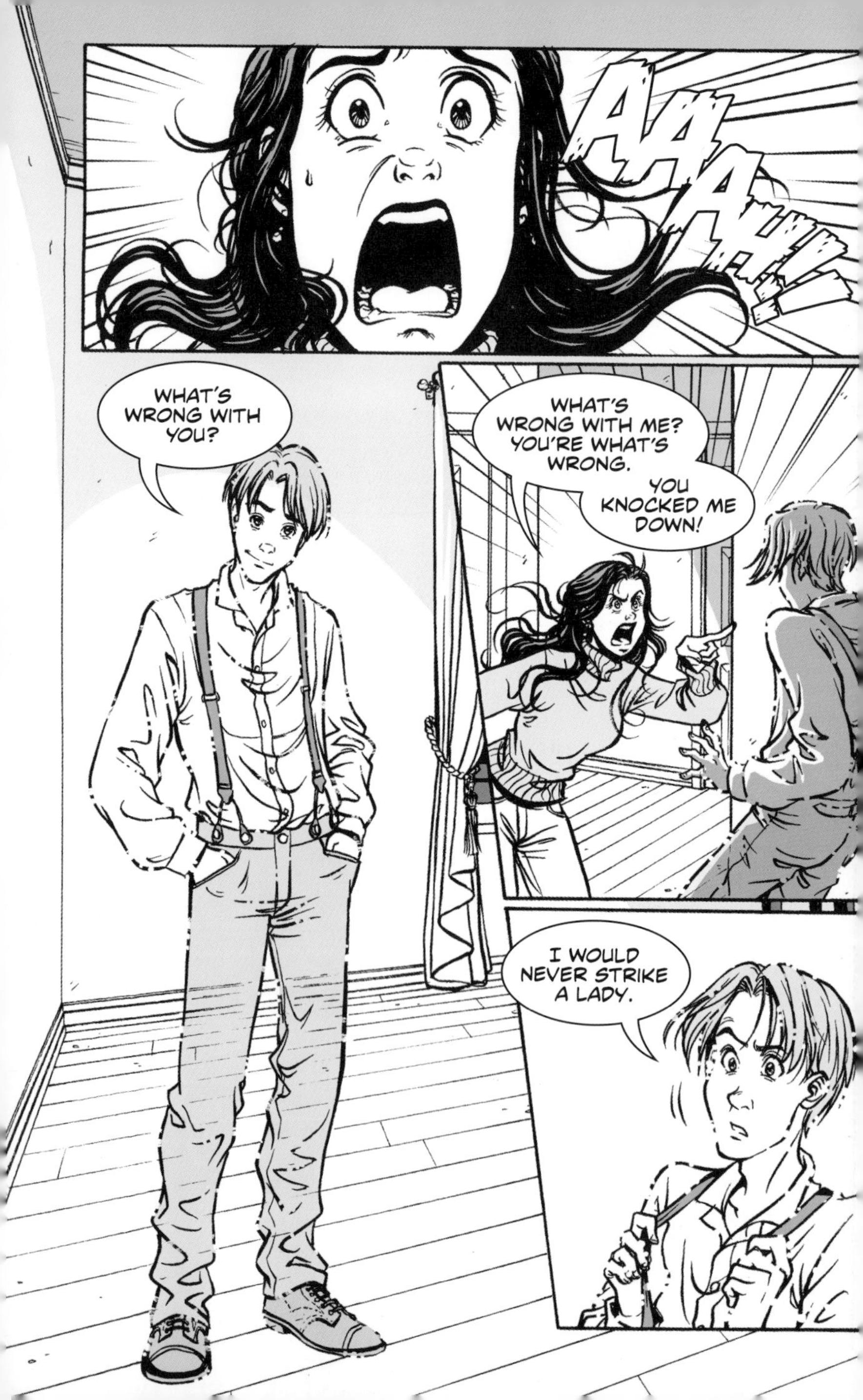
AAAAHH!!!
WHAT'S WRONG WITH YOU?
WHAT'S WRONG WITH ME? YOU'RE WHAT'S WRONG.
YOU KNOCKED ME DOWN!
I WOULD NEVER STRIKE A LADY.

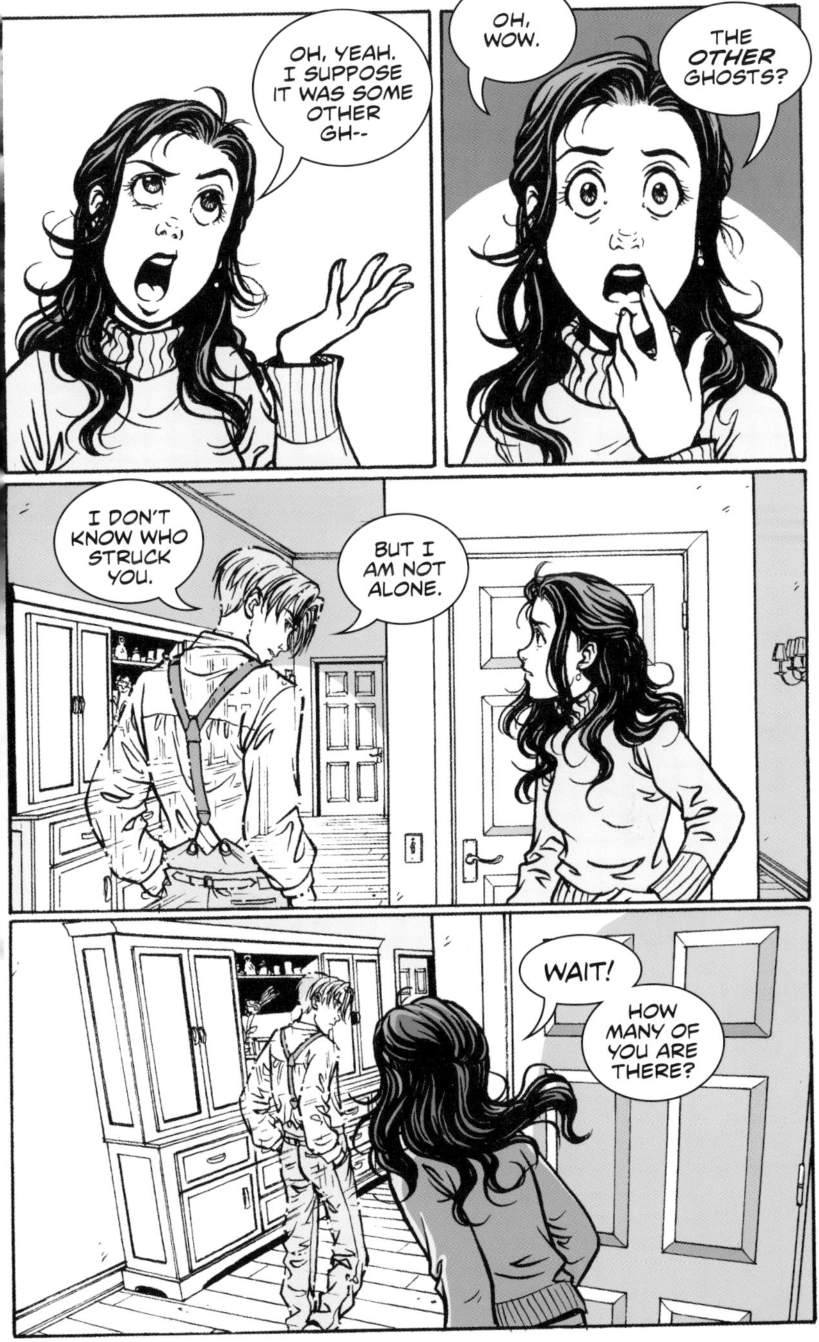
OH, YEAH. I SUPPOSE IT WAS SOME OTHER GH--
OH, WOW.
THE OTHER GHOSTS?
I DON'T KNOW WHO STRUCK YOU.
BUT I AM NOT ALONE.
WAIT!
HOW MANY OF YOU ARE THERE?

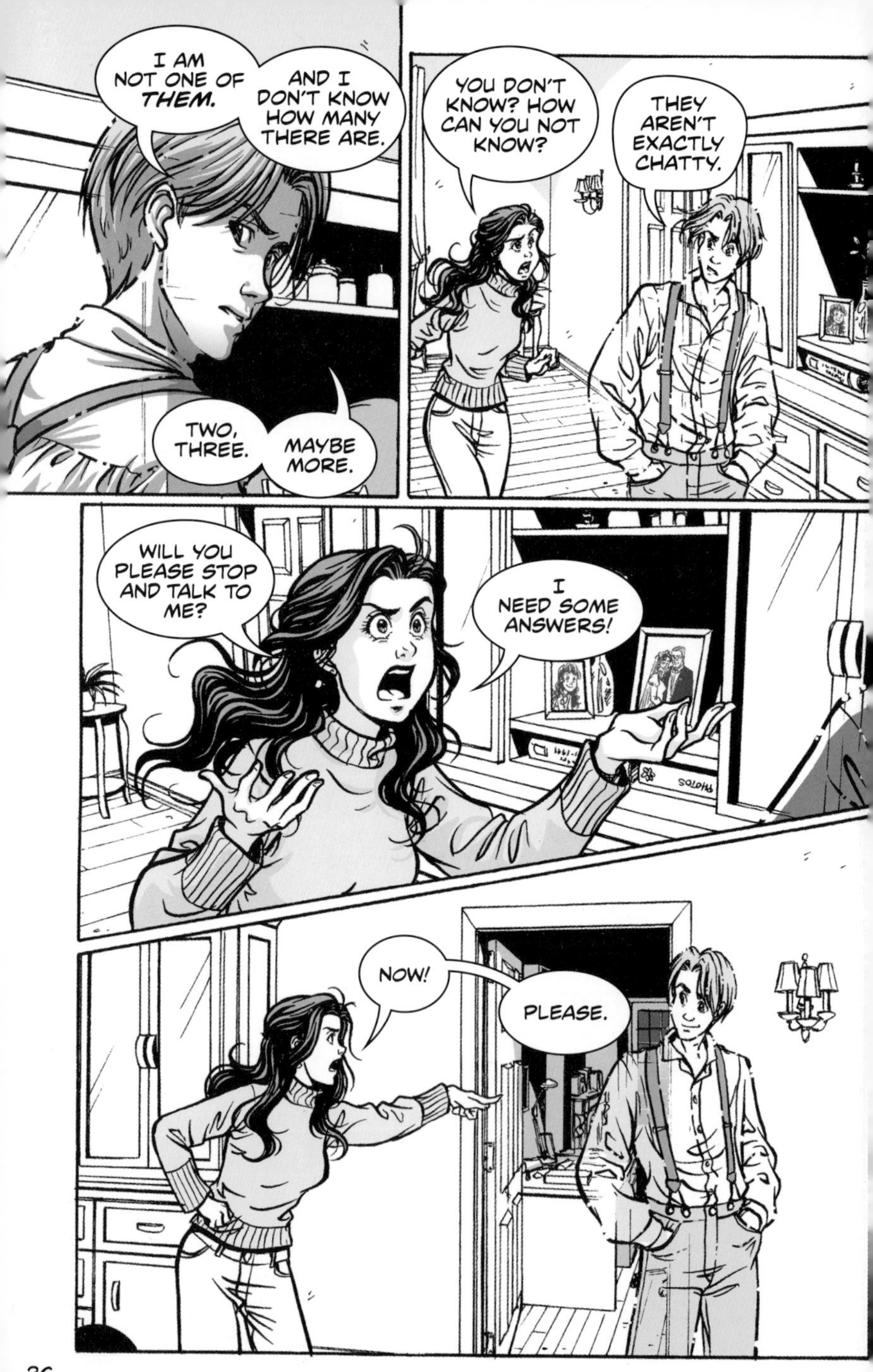
I AM NOT ONE OF *THEM.*
AND I DON'T KNOW HOW MANY THERE ARE.
TWO, THREE.
MAYBE MORE.
YOU DON'T KNOW? HOW CAN YOU NOT KNOW?
THEY AREN'T EXACTLY CHATTY.
WILL YOU PLEASE STOP AND TALK TO ME?
I NEED SOME ANSWERS!
NOW!
PLEASE.

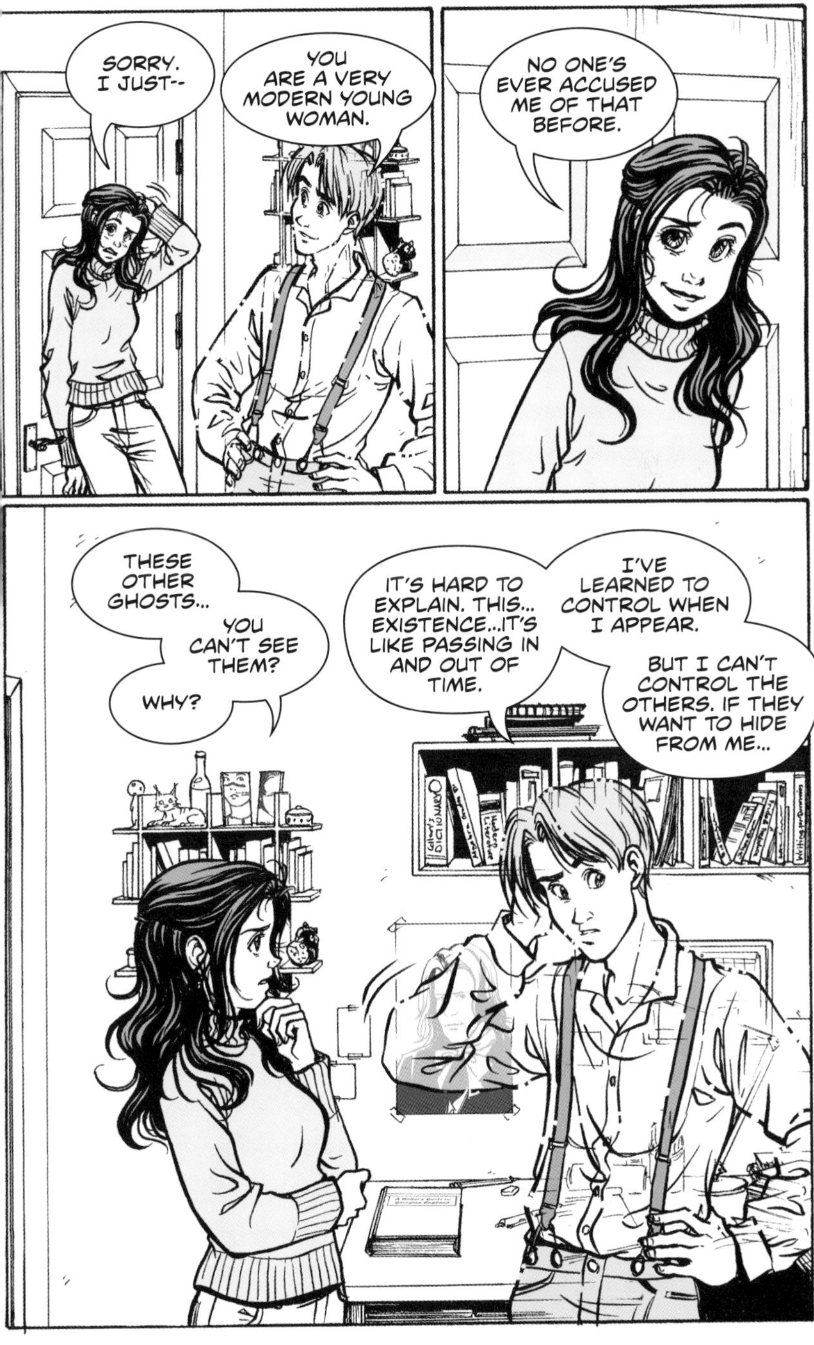
SORRY. I JUST--
YOU ARE A VERY MODERN YOUNG WOMAN.
NO ONE'S EVER ACCUSED ME OF THAT BEFORE.
THESE OTHER GHOSTS...
YOU CAN'T SEE THEM?
WHY?
IT'S HARD TO EXPLAIN. THIS... EXISTENCE...IT'S LIKE PASSING IN AND OUT OF TIME.
I'VE LEARNED TO CONTROL WHEN I APPEAR.
BUT I CAN'T CONTROL THE OTHERS. IF THEY WANT TO HIDE FROM ME...

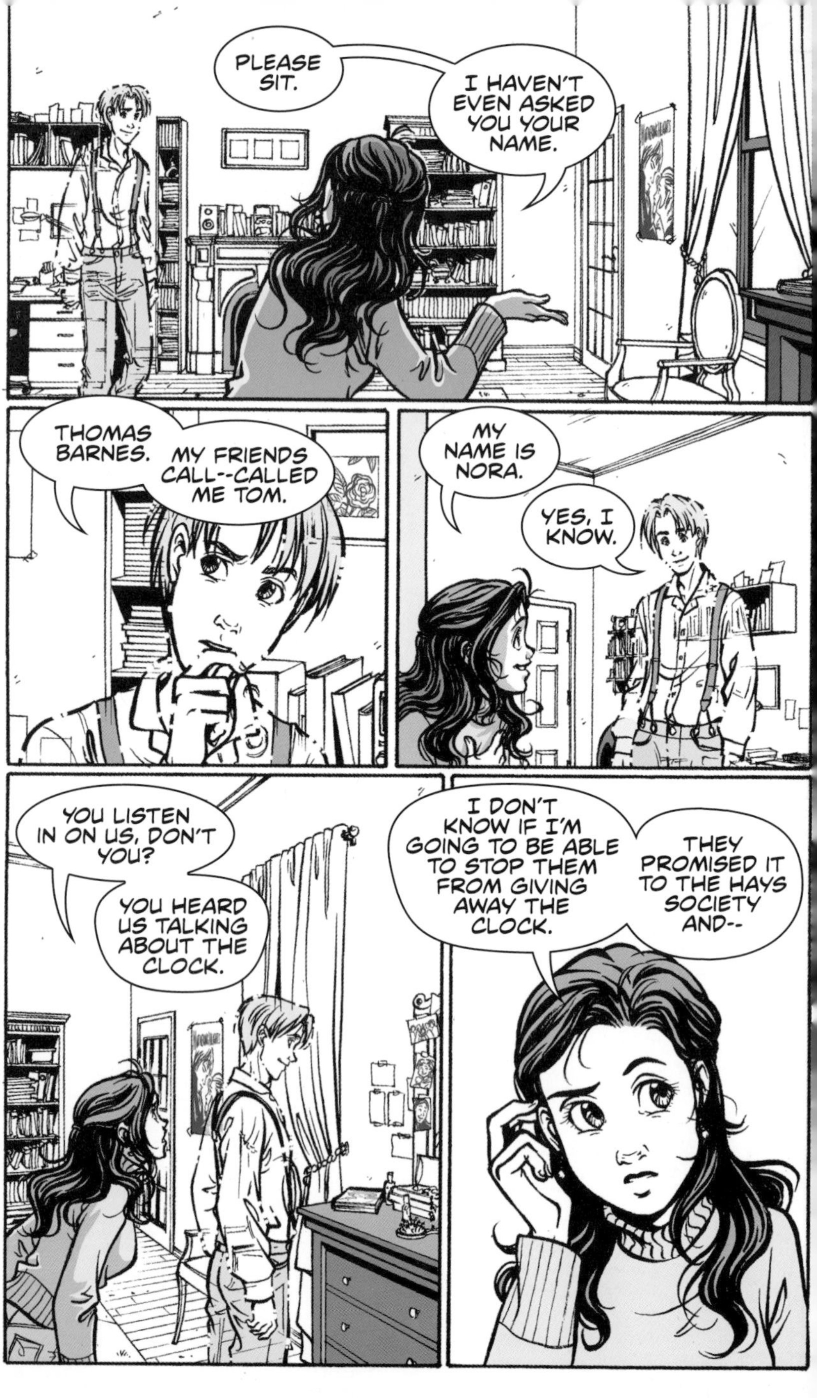
PLEASE SIT.
I HAVEN'T EVEN ASKED YOU YOUR NAME.
THOMAS BARNES.
MY FRIENDS CALL--CALLED ME TOM.
MY NAME IS NORA.
YES, I KNOW.
YOU LISTEN IN ON US, DON'T YOU?
YOU HEARD US TALKING ABOUT THE CLOCK.
I DON'T KNOW IF I'M GOING TO BE ABLE TO STOP THEM FROM GIVING AWAY THE CLOCK.
THEY PROMISED IT TO THE HAYS SOCIETY AND--

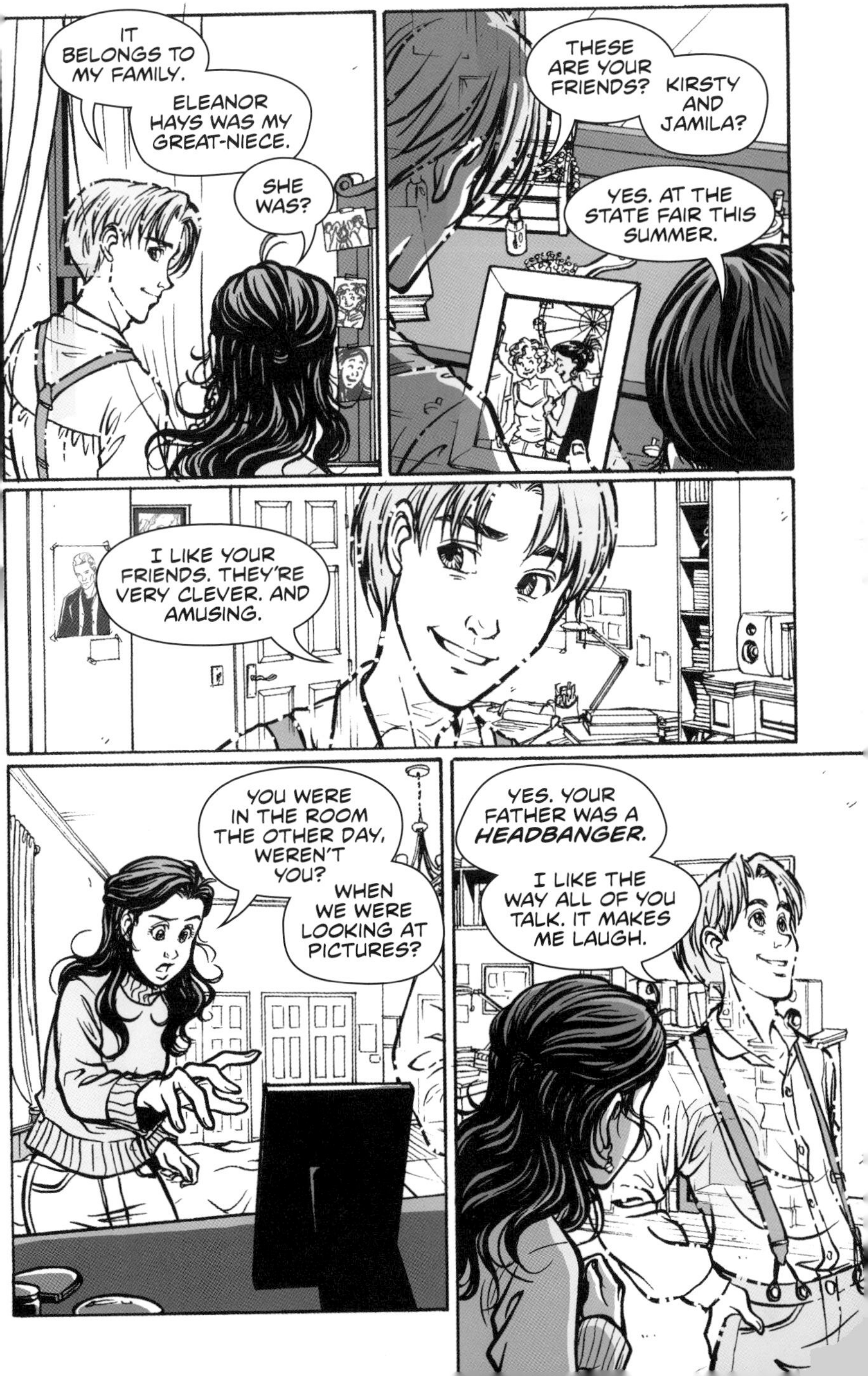
IT BELONGS TO MY FAMILY.
ELEANOR HAYS WAS MY GREAT-NIECE.
SHE WAS?
THESE ARE YOUR FRIENDS?
KIRSTY AND JAMILA?
YES. AT THE STATE FAIR THIS SUMMER.
I LIKE YOUR FRIENDS. THEY'RE VERY CLEVER. AND AMUSING.
YOU WERE IN THE ROOM THE OTHER DAY, WEREN'T YOU?
WHEN WE WERE LOOKING AT PICTURES?
YES. YOUR FATHER WAS A ***HEADBANGER.***
I LIKE THE WAY ALL OF YOU TALK. IT MAKES ME LAUGH.

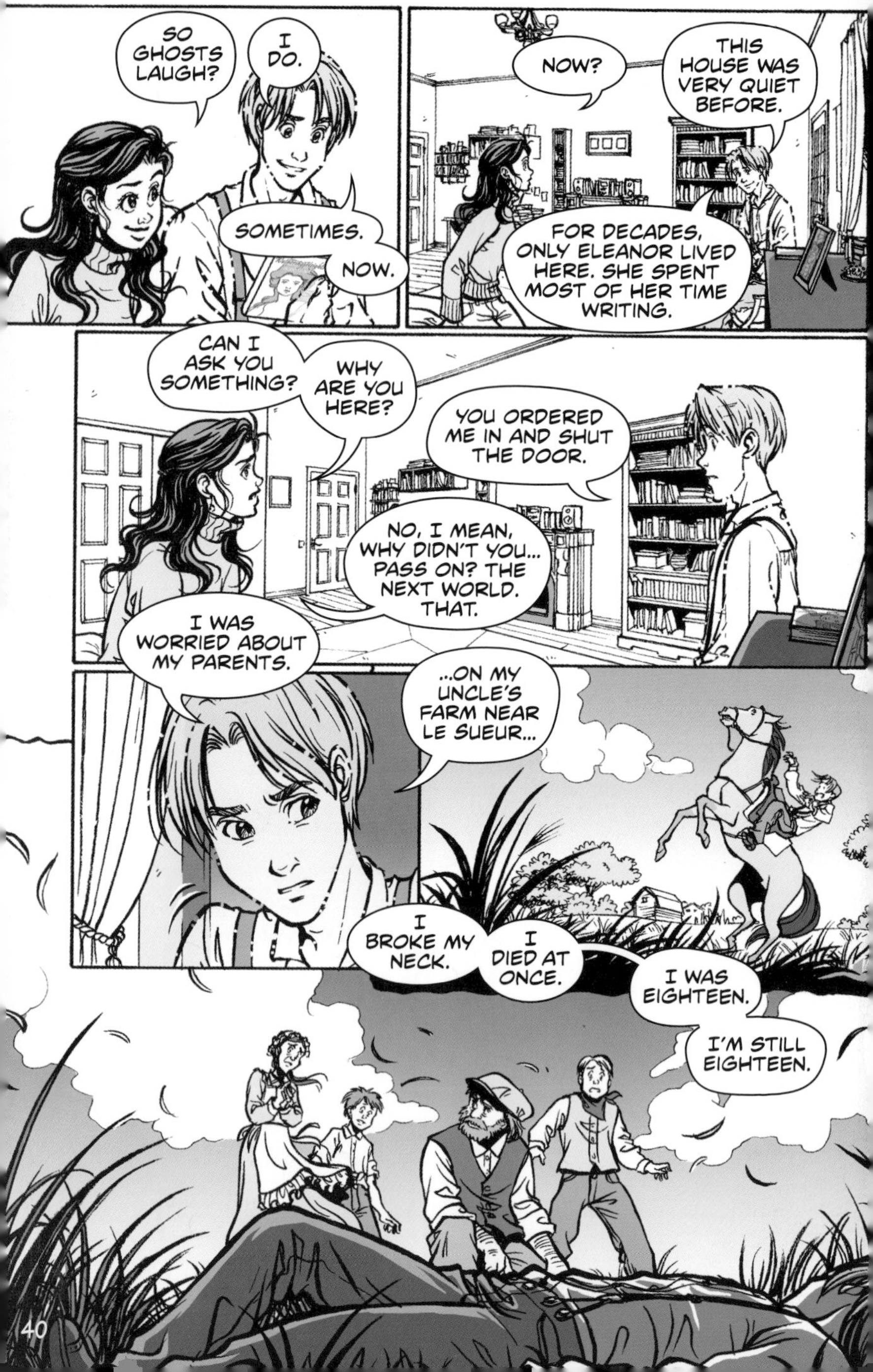
SO GHOSTS LAUGH?
I DO.
SOMETIMES.
NOW.
NOW?
THIS HOUSE WAS VERY QUIET BEFORE.
FOR DECADES, ONLY ELEANOR LIVED HERE. SHE SPENT MOST OF HER TIME WRITING.
CAN I ASK YOU SOMETHING?
WHY ARE YOU HERE?
YOU ORDERED ME IN AND SHUT THE DOOR.
NO, I MEAN, WHY DIDN'T YOU... PASS ON? THE NEXT WORLD. THAT.
I WAS WORRIED ABOUT MY PARENTS.
...ON MY UNCLE'S FARM NEAR LE SUEUR...
I BROKE MY NECK.
I DIED AT ONCE.
I WAS EIGHTEEN.
I'M STILL EIGHTEEN.

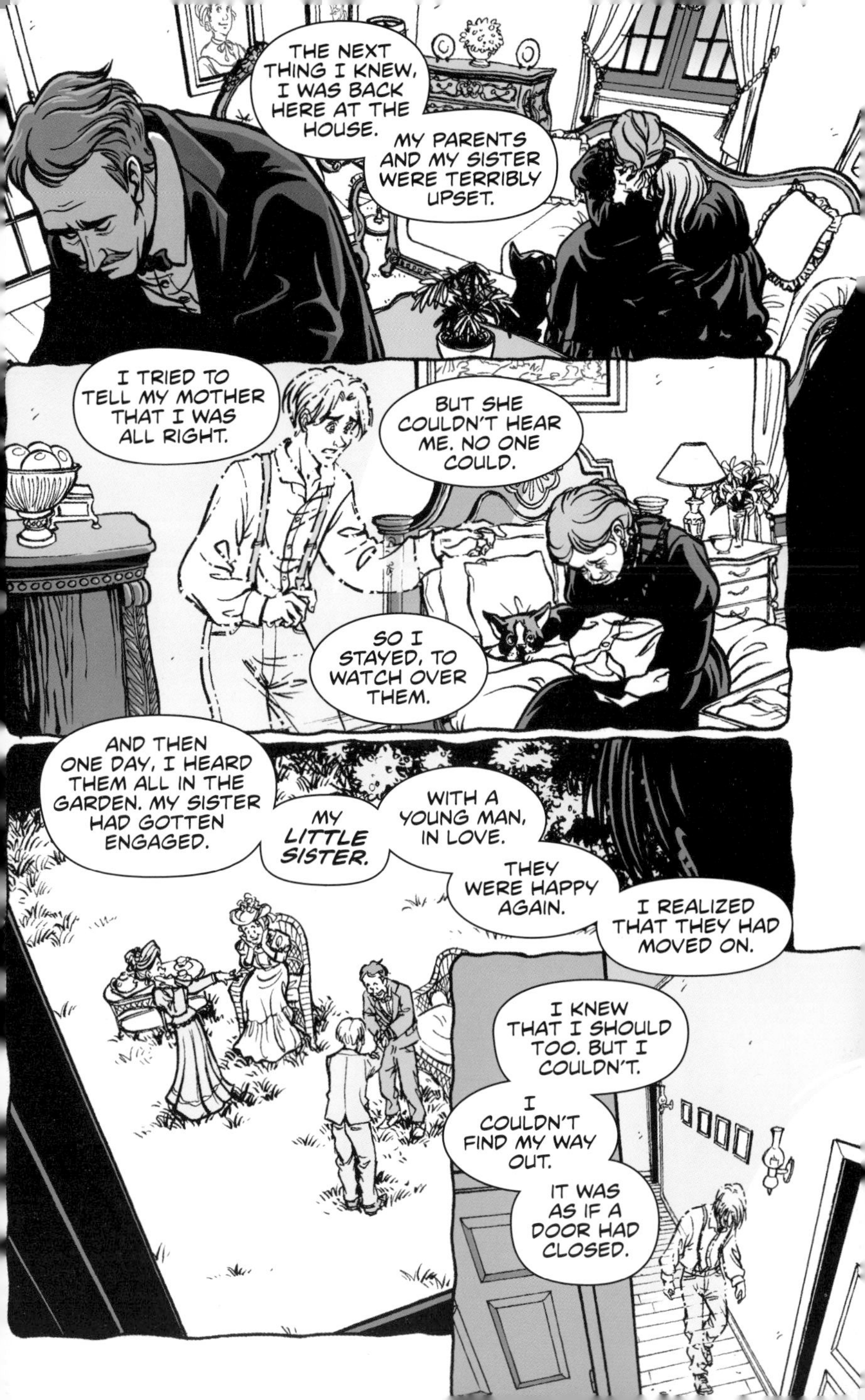
THE NEXT THING I KNEW, I WAS BACK HERE AT THE HOUSE.
MY PARENTS AND MY SISTER WERE TERRIBLY UPSET.
I TRIED TO TELL MY MOTHER THAT I WAS ALL RIGHT.
BUT SHE COULDN'T HEAR ME. NO ONE COULD.
SO I STAYED, TO WATCH OVER THEM.
AND THEN ONE DAY, I HEARD THEM ALL IN THE GARDEN. MY SISTER HAD GOTTEN ENGAGED.
MY *LITTLE SISTER.*
WITH A YOUNG MAN, IN LOVE.
THEY WERE HAPPY AGAIN.
I REALIZED THAT THEY HAD MOVED ON.
I KNEW THAT I SHOULD TOO. BUT I COULDN'T.
I COULDN'T FIND MY WAY OUT.
IT WAS AS IF A DOOR HAD CLOSED.

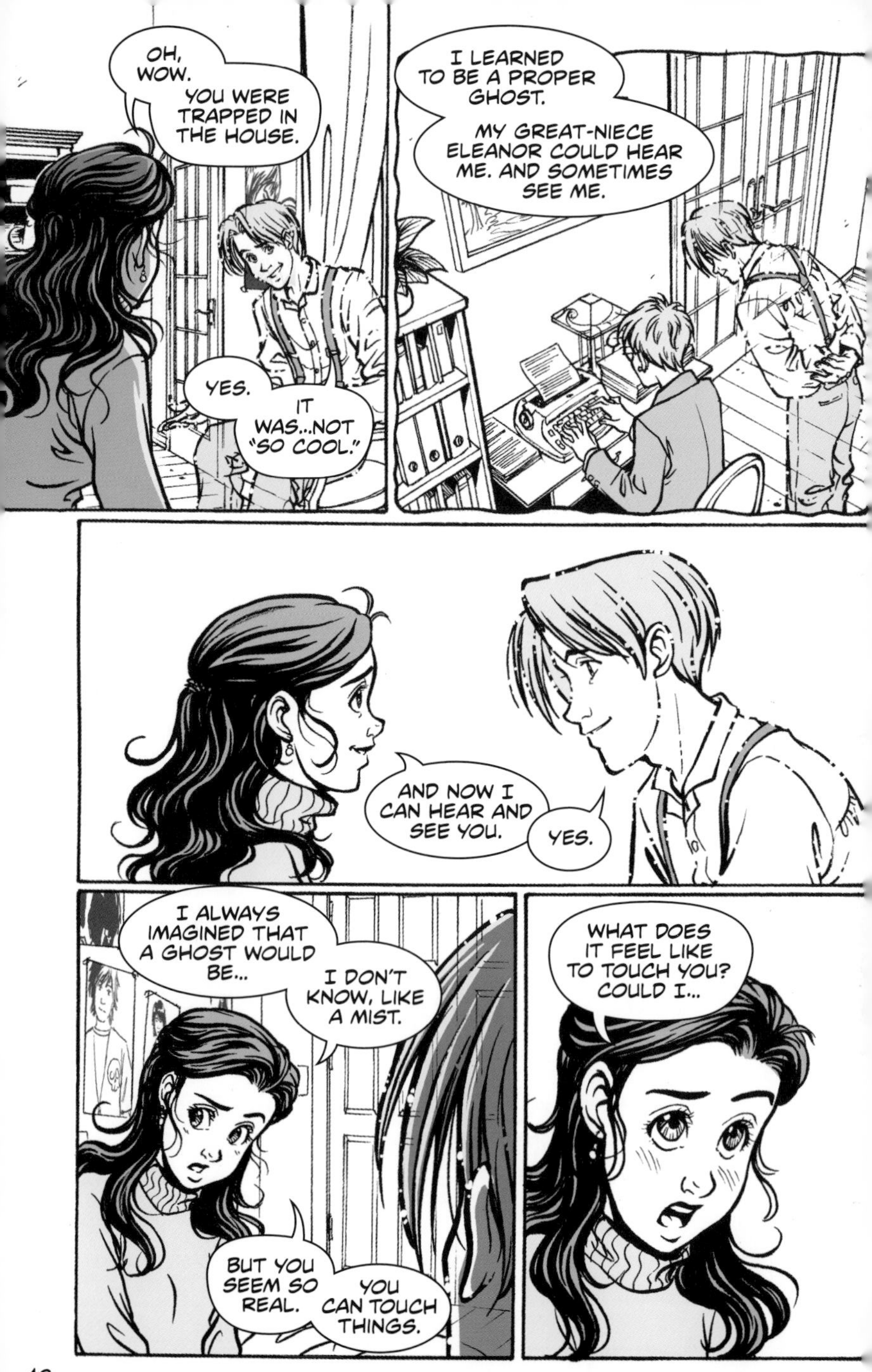
OH, WOW.
YOU WERE TRAPPED IN THE HOUSE.
YES.
IT WAS...NOT "SO COOL."
I LEARNED TO BE A PROPER GHOST.
MY GREAT-NIECE ELEANOR COULD HEAR ME. AND SOMETIMES SEE ME.
AND NOW I CAN HEAR AND SEE YOU.
YES.
I ALWAYS IMAGINED THAT A GHOST WOULD BE...
I DON'T KNOW, LIKE A MIST.
BUT YOU SEEM SO REAL.
YOU CAN TOUCH THINGS.
WHAT DOES IT FEEL LIKE TO TOUCH YOU? COULD I...

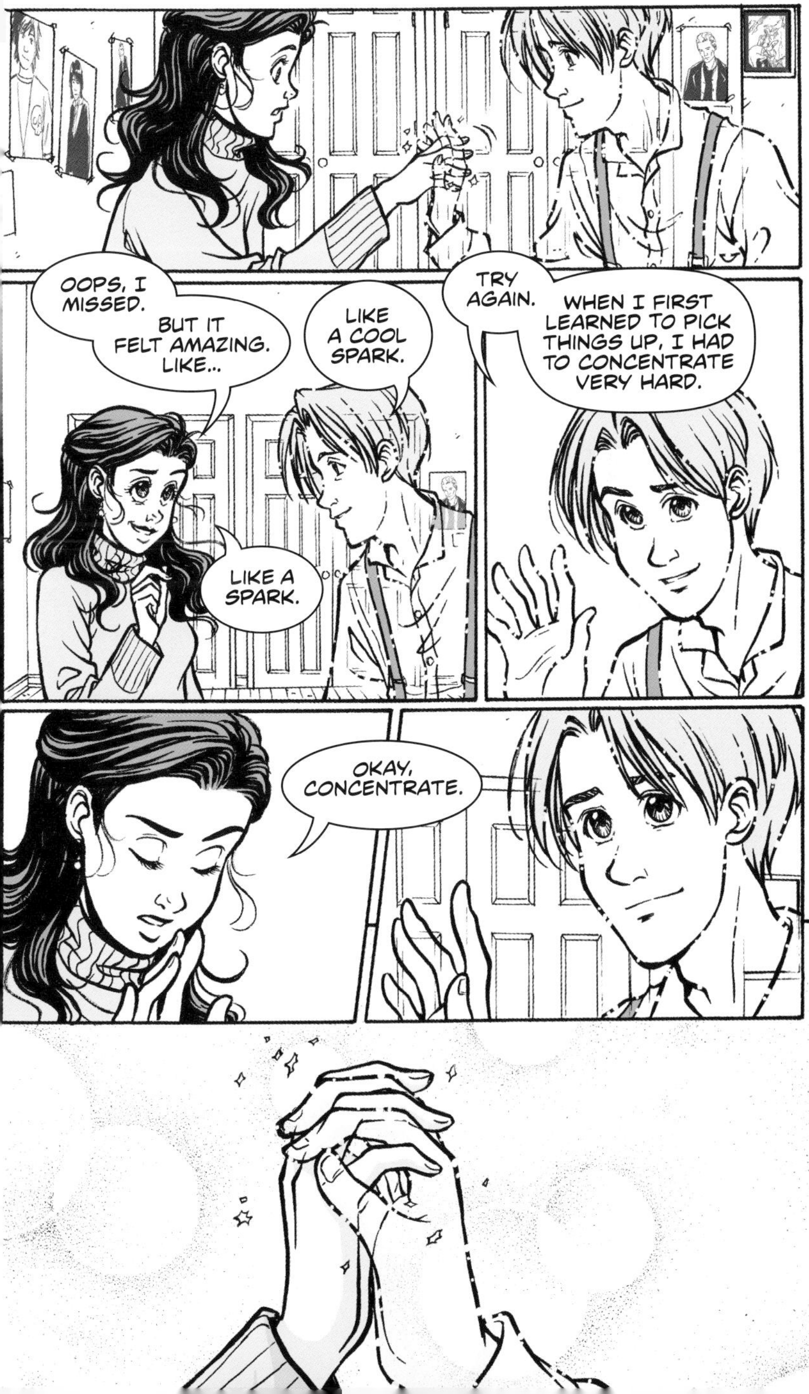
OOPS, I MISSED.
BUT IT FELT AMAZING. LIKE...
LIKE A COOL SPARK.
LIKE A SPARK.
TRY AGAIN.
WHEN I FIRST LEARNED TO PICK THINGS UP, I HAD TO CONCENTRATE VERY HARD.
OKAY, CONCENTRATE.

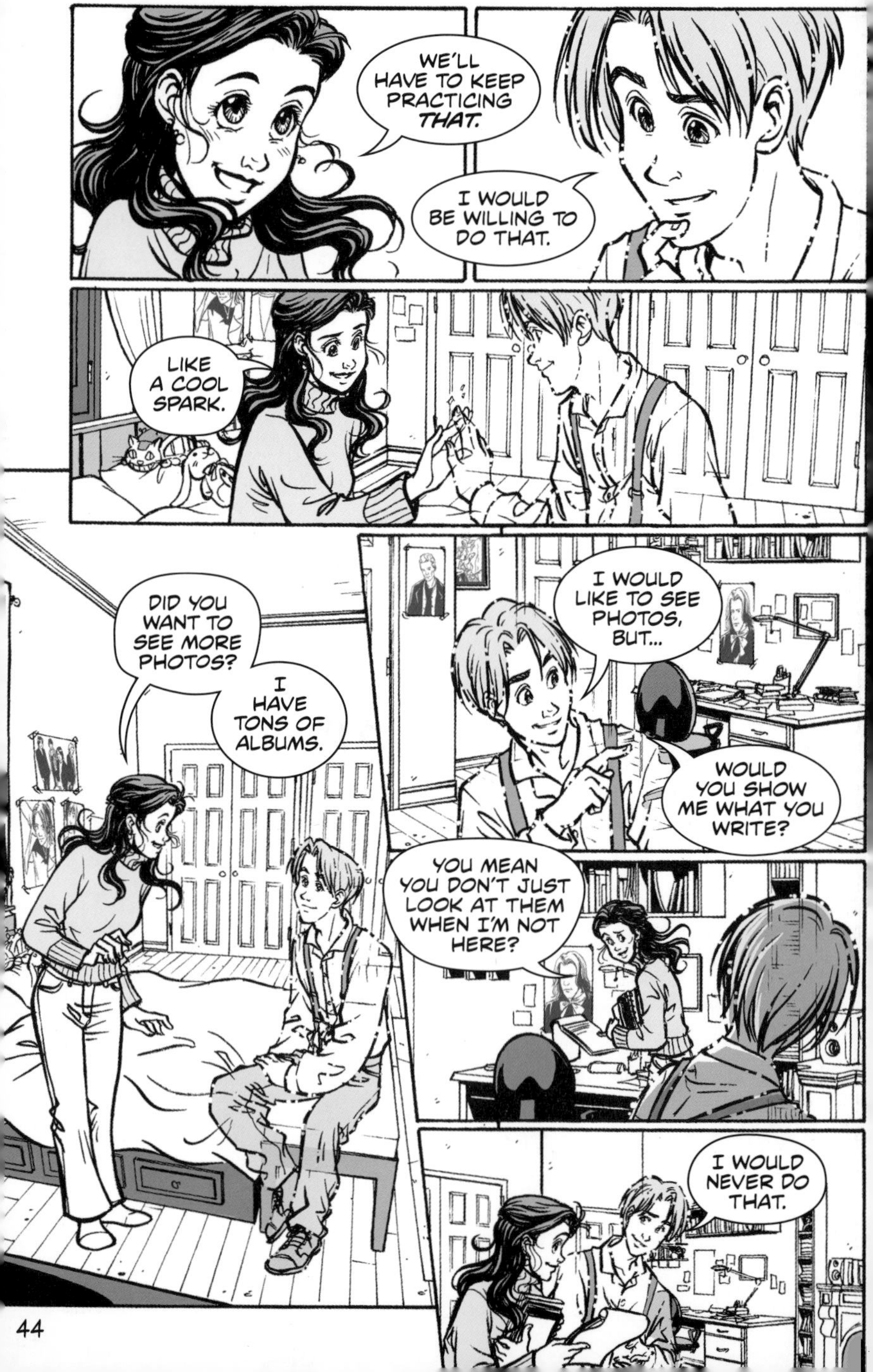
WE'LL HAVE TO KEEP PRACTICING THAT.
I WOULD BE WILLING TO DO THAT.
LIKE A COOL SPARK.
DID YOU WANT TO SEE MORE PHOTOS?
I HAVE TONS OF ALBUMS.
I WOULD LIKE TO SEE PHOTOS, BUT...
WOULD YOU SHOW ME WHAT YOU WRITE?
YOU MEAN YOU DON'T JUST LOOK AT THEM WHEN I'M NOT HERE?
I WOULD NEVER DO THAT.

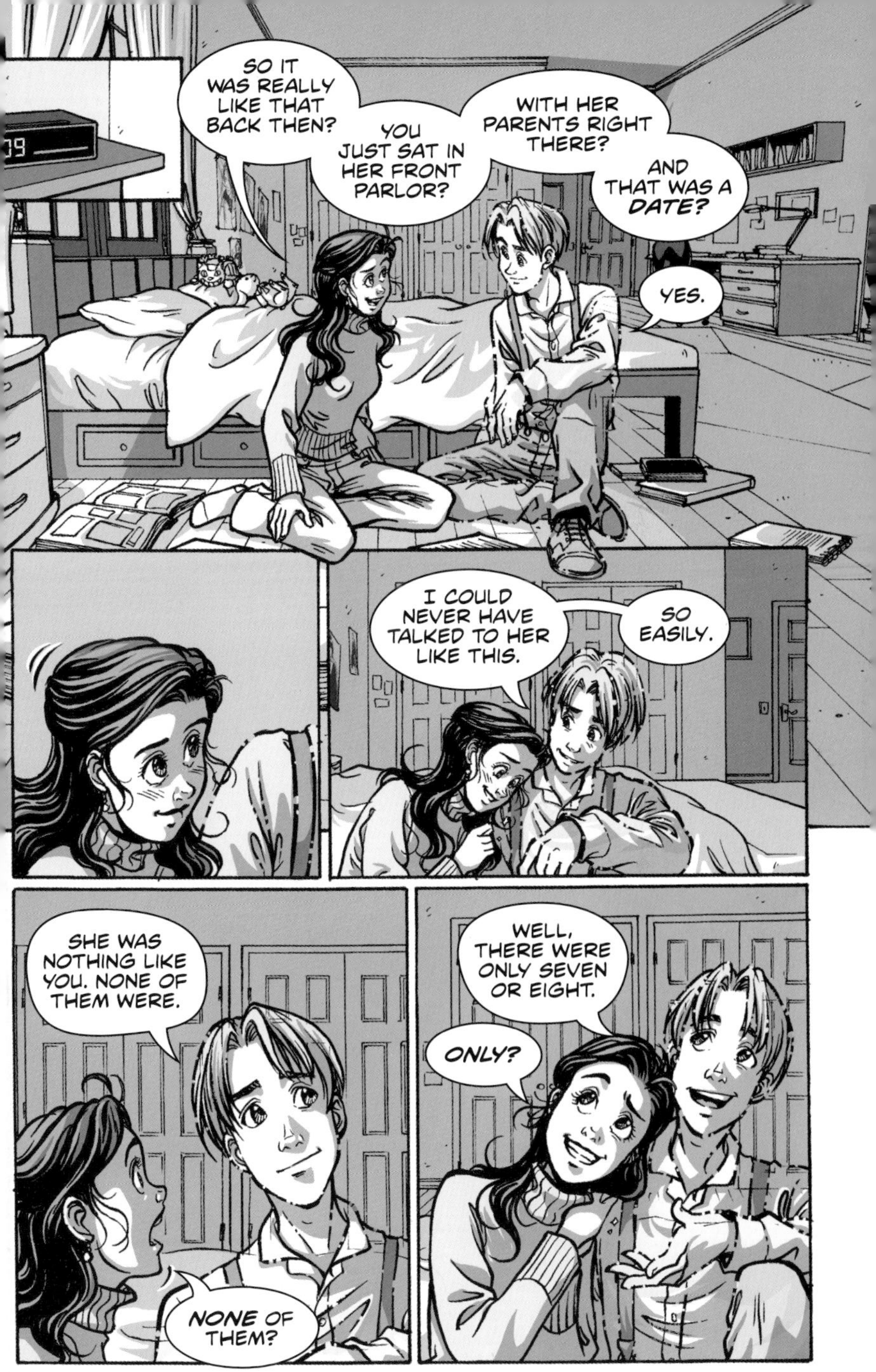
SO IT WAS REALLY LIKE THAT BACK THEN?
YOU JUST SAT IN HER FRONT PARLOR?
WITH HER PARENTS RIGHT THERE?
AND THAT WAS A DATE?
YES.
I COULD NEVER HAVE TALKED TO HER LIKE THIS.
SO EASILY.
SHE WAS NOTHING LIKE YOU. NONE OF THEM WERE.
NONE OF THEM?
WELL, THERE WERE ONLY SEVEN OR EIGHT.
ONLY?

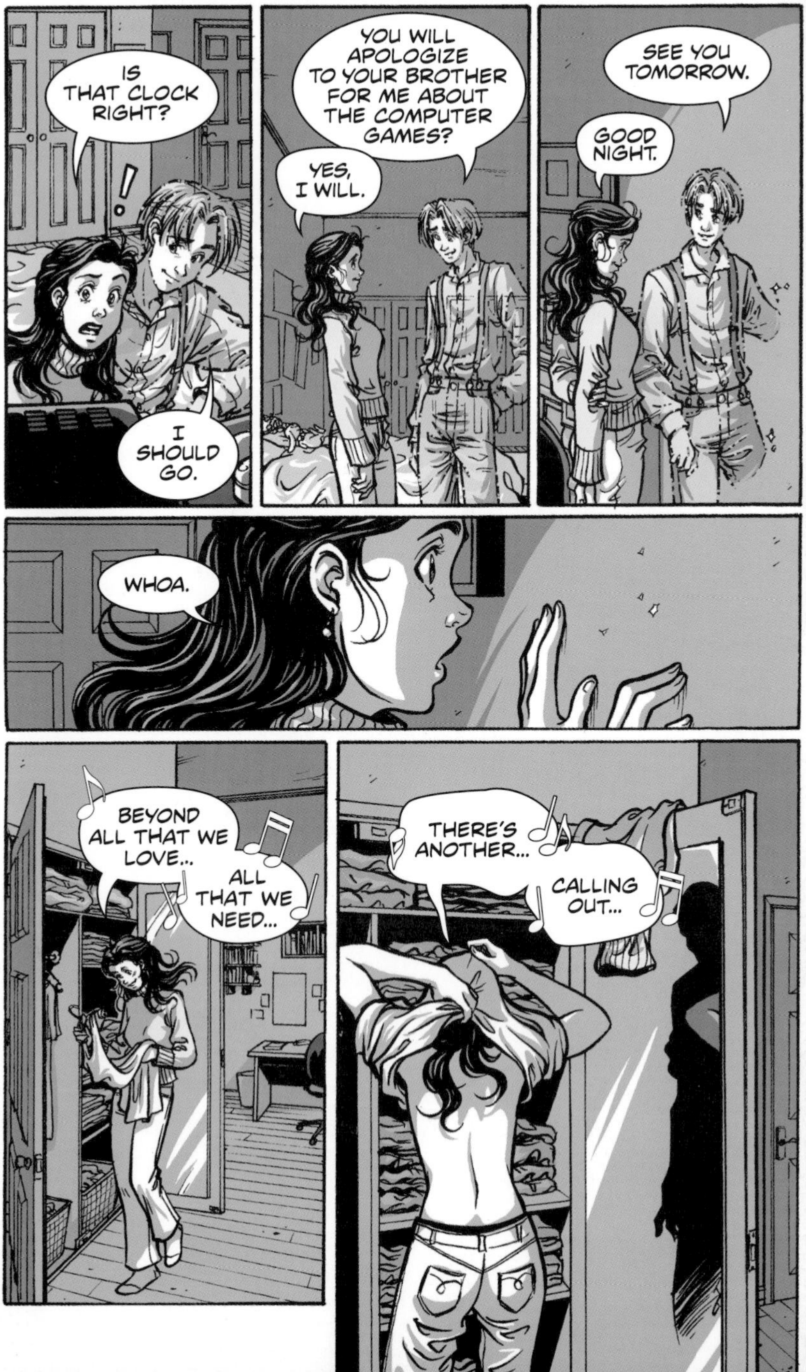
IS THAT CLOCK RIGHT?
!
I SHOULD GO.
YOU WILL APOLOGIZE TO YOUR BROTHER FOR ME ABOUT THE COMPUTER GAMES?
YES, I WILL.
SEE YOU TOMORROW.
GOOD NIGHT.
WHOA.
BEYOND ALL THAT WE LOVE...
ALL THAT WE NEED...
THERE'S ANOTHER...
CALLING OUT...

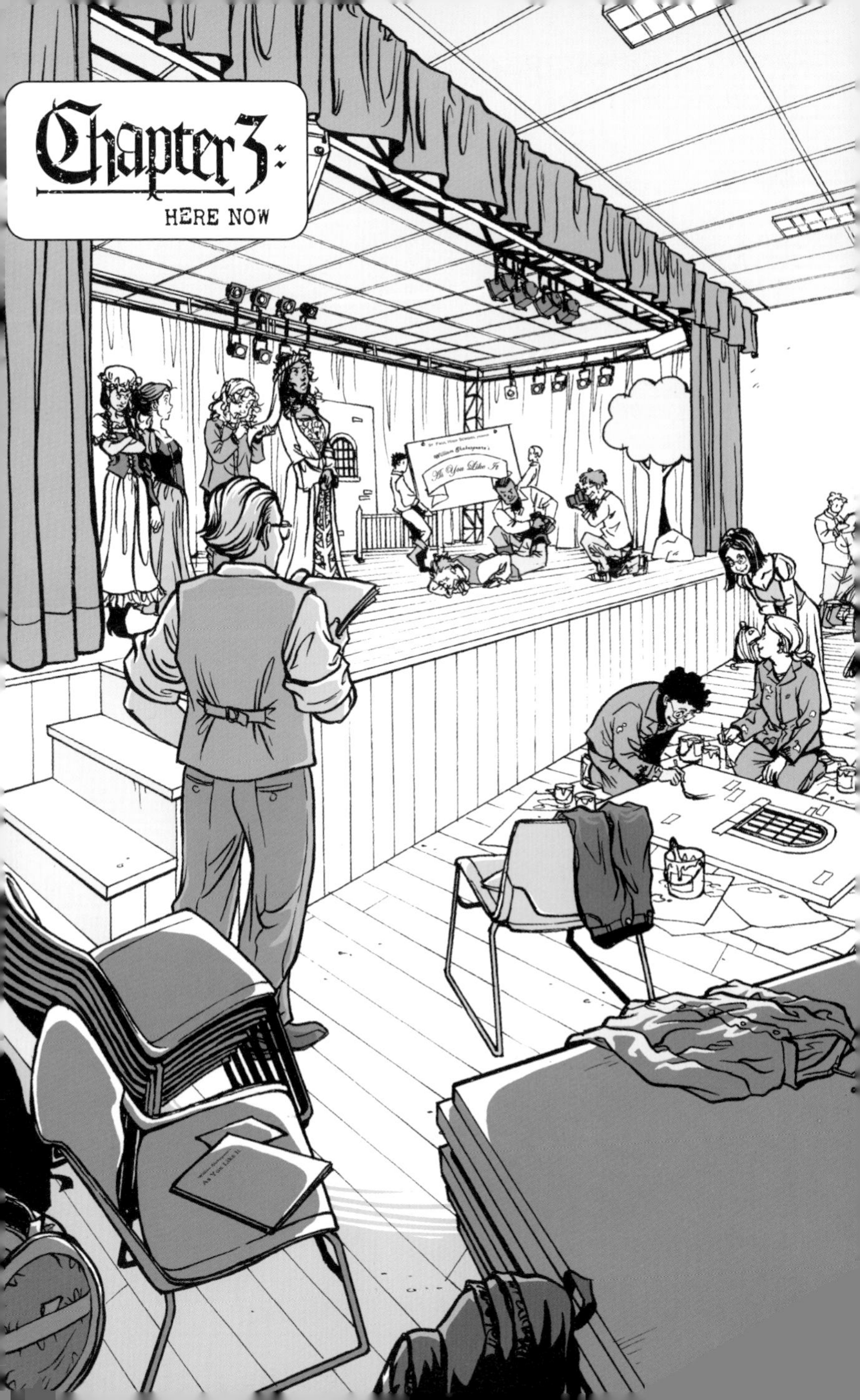

Chapter 3:
HERE NOW
William Shakespeare's
As You Like It
As You Like It

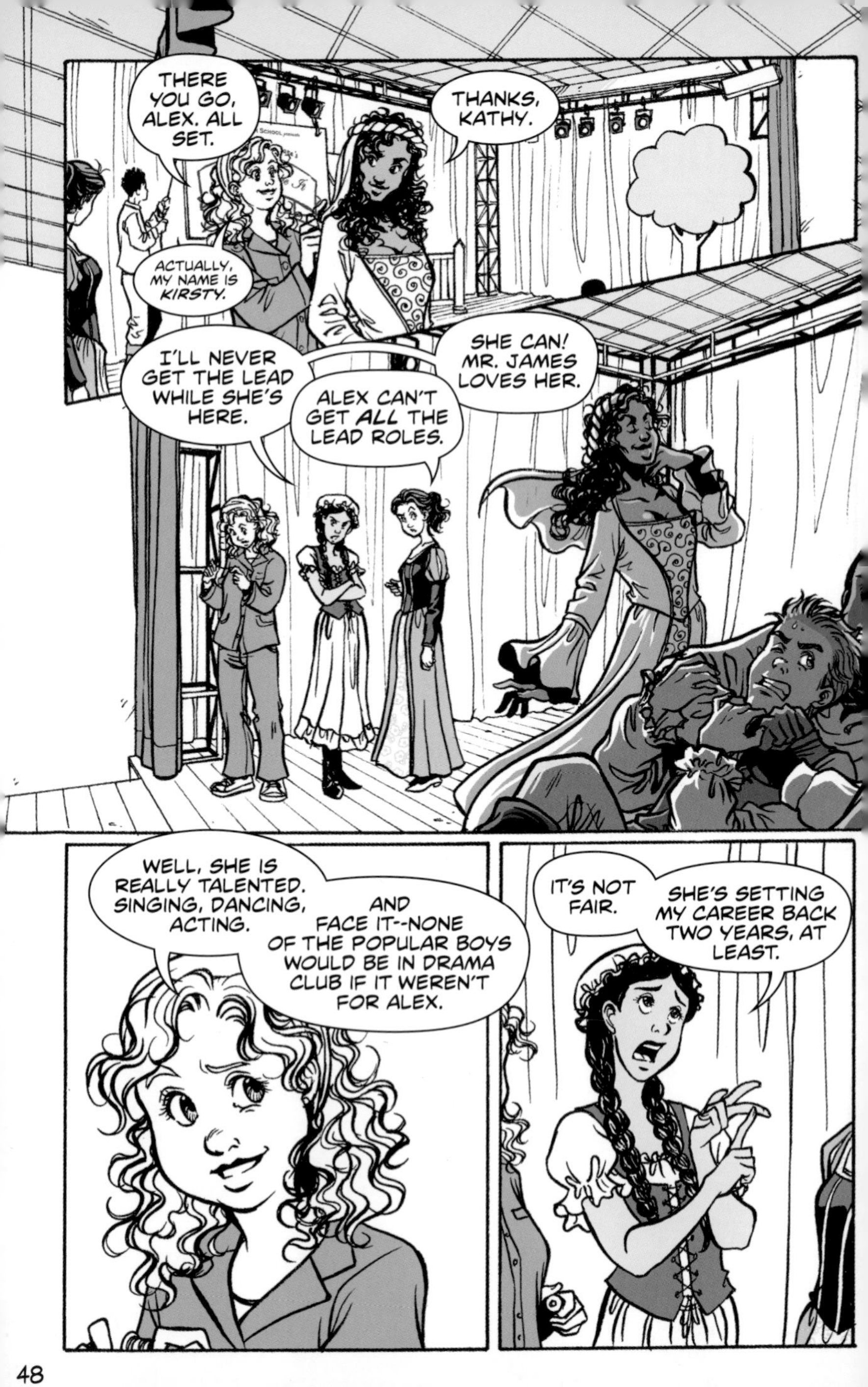

THERE YOU GO, ALEX. ALL SET.
THANKS, KATHY.
ACTUALLY, MY NAME IS *KIRSTY.*
I'LL NEVER GET THE LEAD WHILE SHE'S HERE.
ALEX CAN'T GET ***ALL*** THE LEAD ROLES.
SHE CAN! MR. JAMES LOVES HER.
WELL, SHE IS REALLY TALENTED. SINGING, DANCING, ACTING.
AND FACE IT--NONE OF THE POPULAR BOYS WOULD BE IN DRAMA CLUB IF IT WEREN'T FOR ALEX.
IT'S NOT FAIR.
SHE'S SETTING MY CAREER BACK TWO YEARS, AT LEAST.

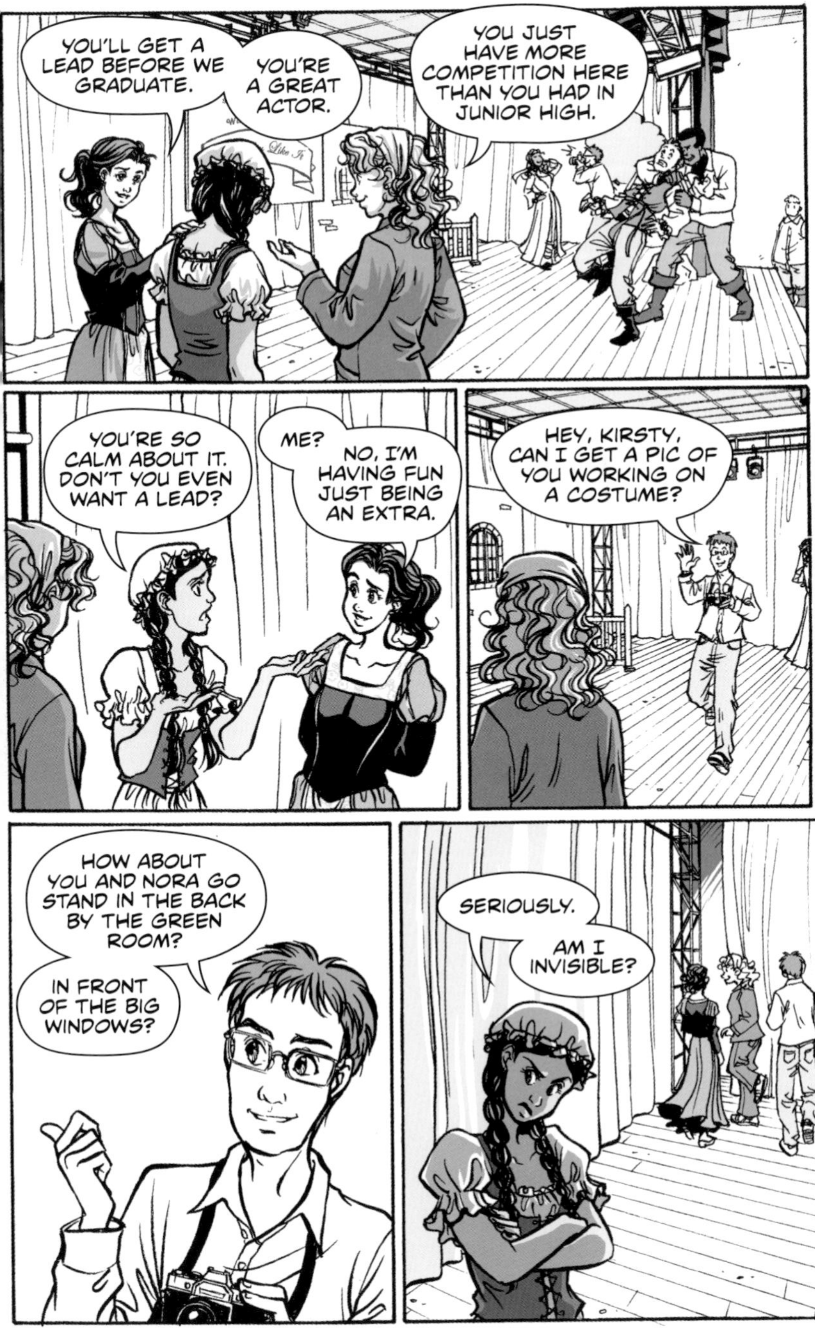

YOU'LL GET A LEAD BEFORE WE GRADUATE.
YOU'RE A GREAT ACTOR.
YOU JUST HAVE MORE COMPETITION HERE THAN YOU HAD IN JUNIOR HIGH.
YOU'RE SO CALM ABOUT IT. DON'T YOU EVEN WANT A LEAD?
ME?
NO, I'M HAVING FUN JUST BEING AN EXTRA.
HEY, KIRSTY, CAN I GET A PIC OF YOU WORKING ON A COSTUME?
HOW ABOUT YOU AND NORA GO STAND IN THE BACK BY THE GREEN ROOM?
IN FRONT OF THE BIG WINDOWS?
SERIOUSLY.
AM I INVISIBLE?

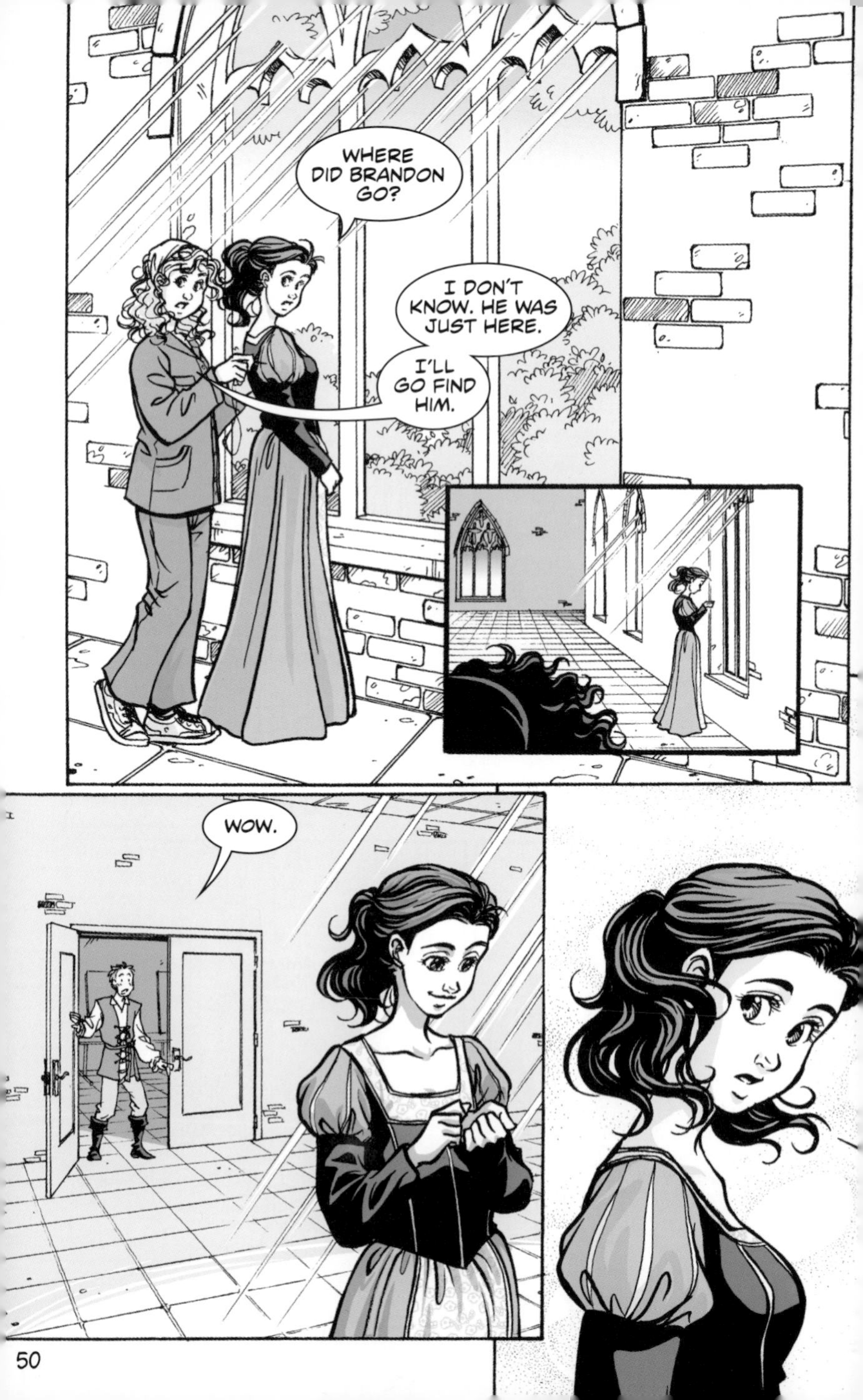
WHERE DID BRANDON GO?
I DON'T KNOW. HE WAS JUST HERE.
I'LL GO FIND HIM.
WOW.

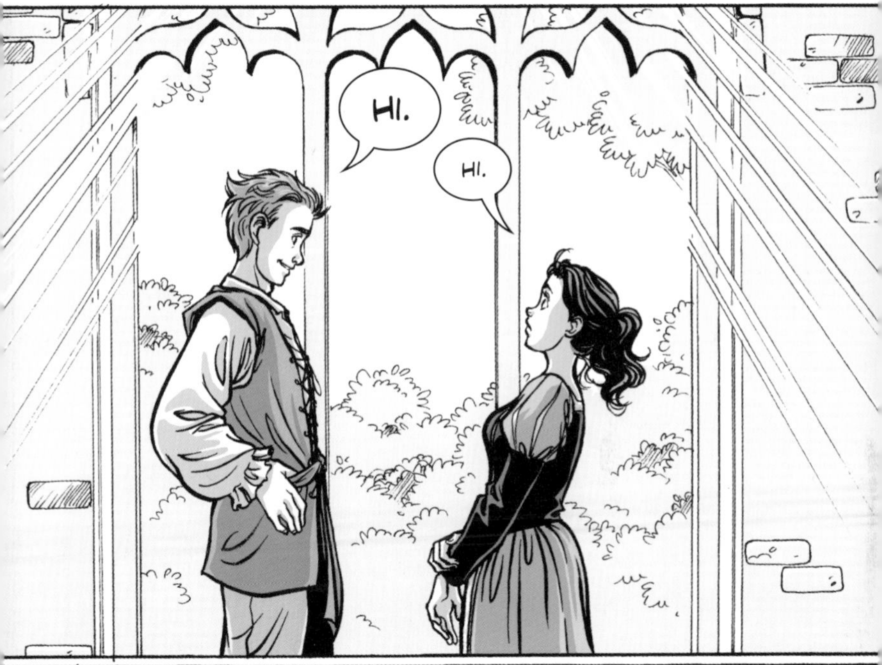
HI.
HI.

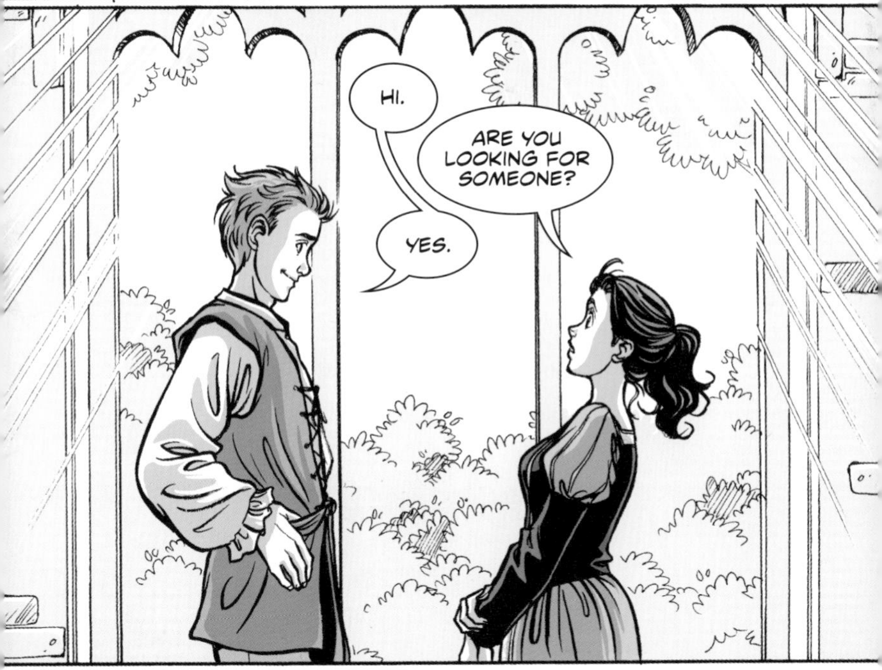
HI.
ARE YOU LOOKING FOR SOMEONE?
YES.

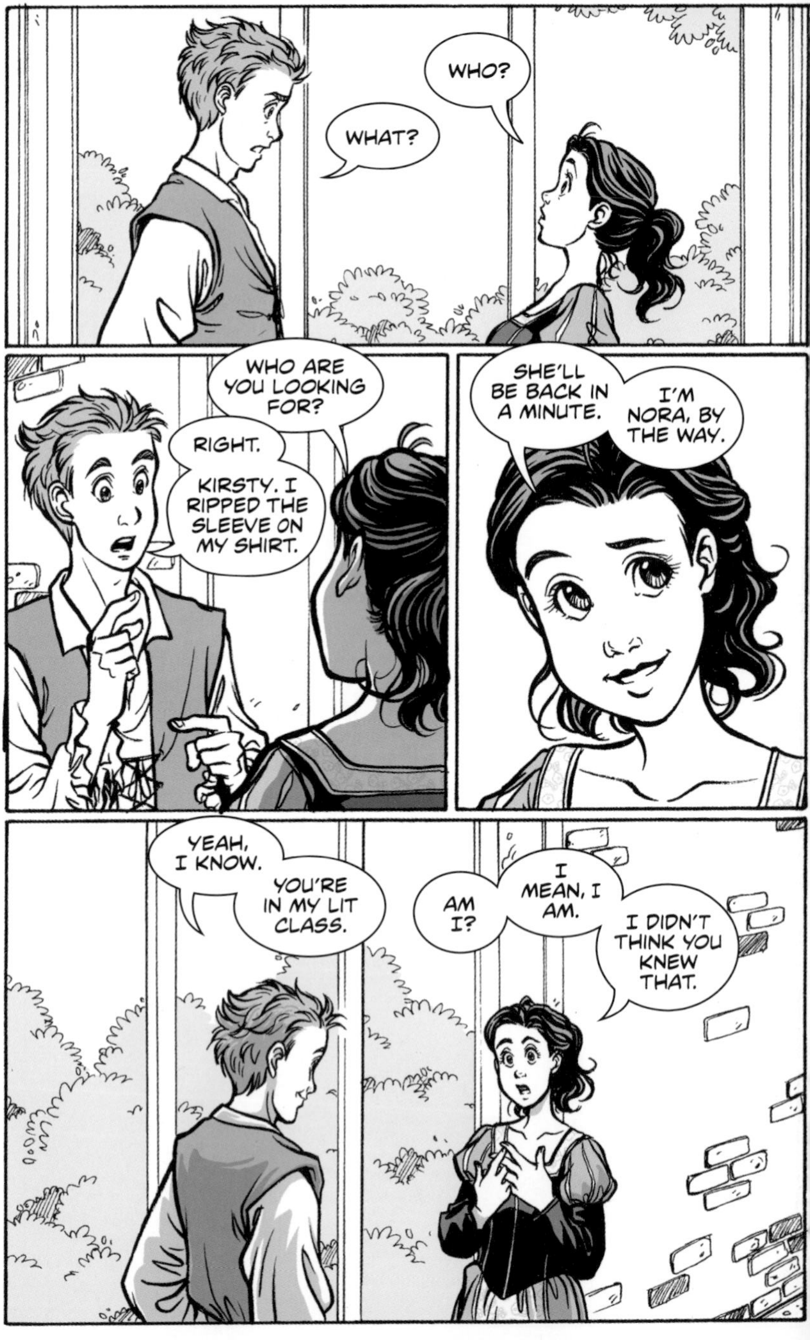
WHAT?
WHO?
WHO ARE YOU LOOKING FOR?
RIGHT.
KIRSTY. I RIPPED THE SLEEVE ON MY SHIRT.
SHE'LL BE BACK IN A MINUTE.
I'M NORA, BY THE WAY.
YEAH, I KNOW.
YOU'RE IN MY LIT CLASS.
AM I?
I MEAN, I AM.
I DIDN'T THINK YOU KNEW THAT.

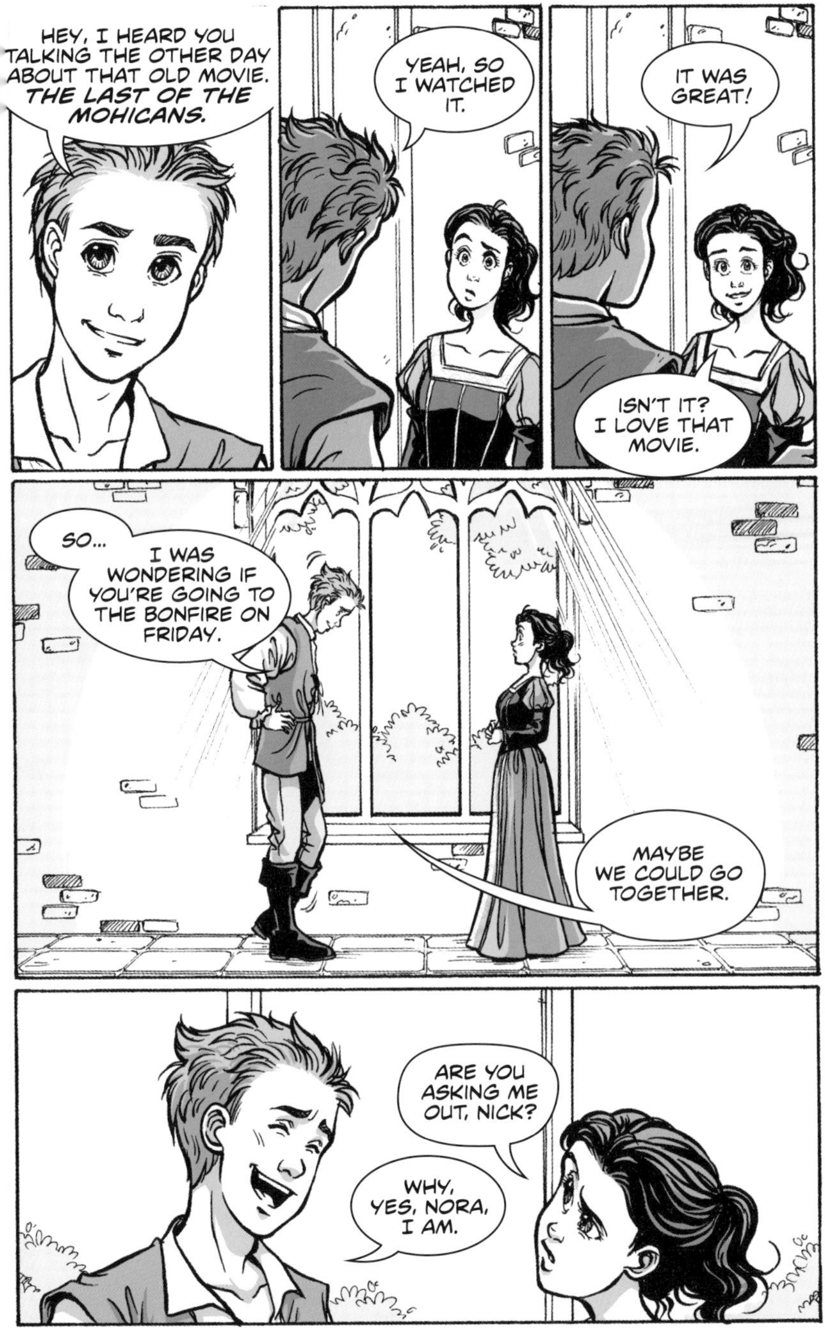
HEY, I HEARD YOU TALKING THE OTHER DAY ABOUT THAT OLD MOVIE. *THE LAST OF THE MOHICANS.*
YEAH, SO I WATCHED IT.
IT WAS GREAT!
ISN'T IT? I LOVE THAT MOVIE.
SO...
I WAS WONDERING IF YOU'RE GOING TO THE BONFIRE ON FRIDAY.
MAYBE WE COULD GO TOGETHER.
ARE YOU ASKING ME OUT, NICK?
WHY, YES, NORA, I AM.

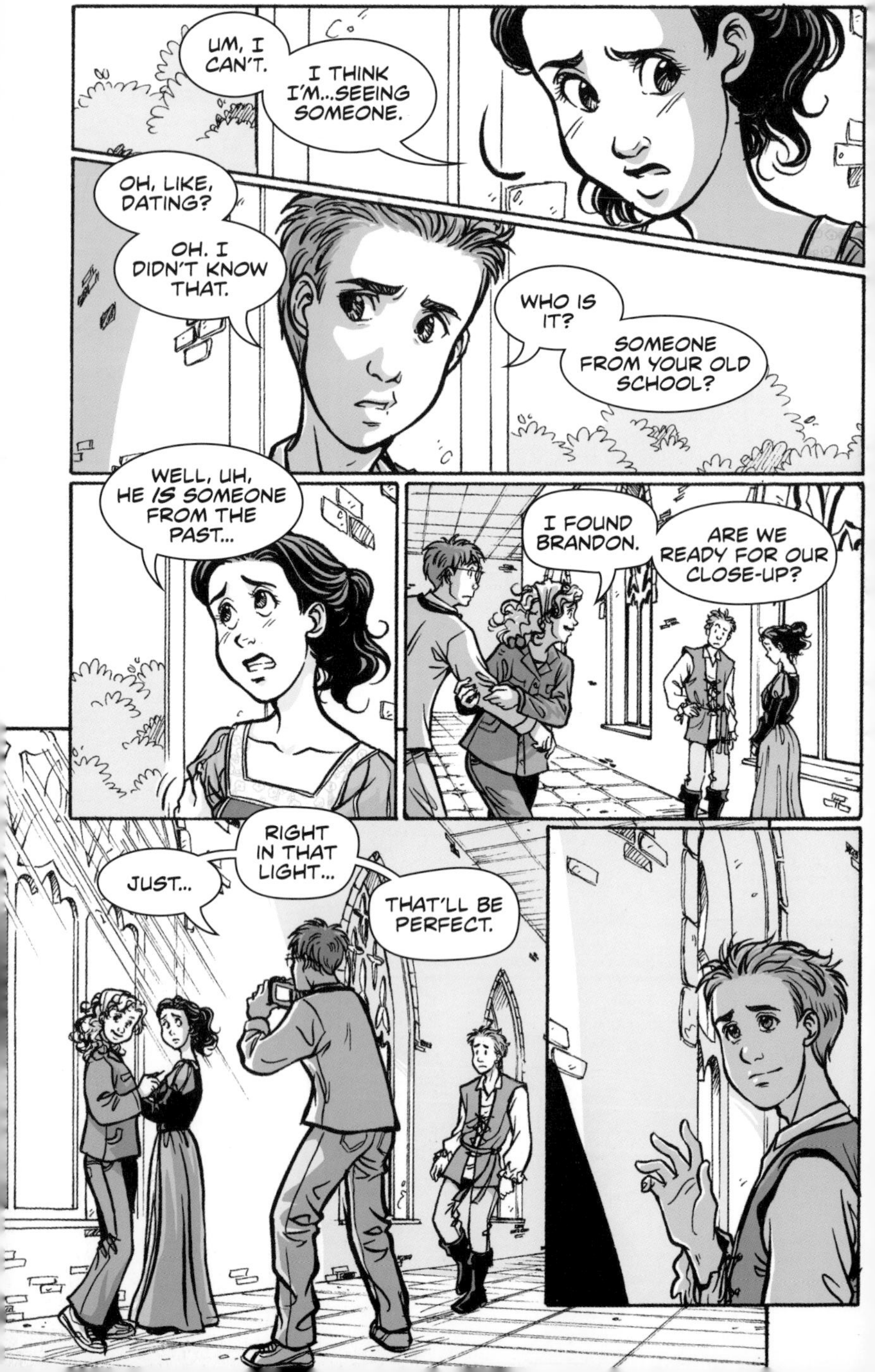
UM, I CAN'T.
I THINK I'M...SEEING SOMEONE.
OH, LIKE, DATING?
OH. I DIDN'T KNOW THAT.
WHO IS IT?
SOMEONE FROM YOUR OLD SCHOOL?
WELL, UH, HE *IS* SOMEONE FROM THE PAST...
I FOUND BRANDON.
ARE WE READY FOR OUR CLOSE-UP?
JUST...
RIGHT IN THAT LIGHT...
THAT'LL BE PERFECT.

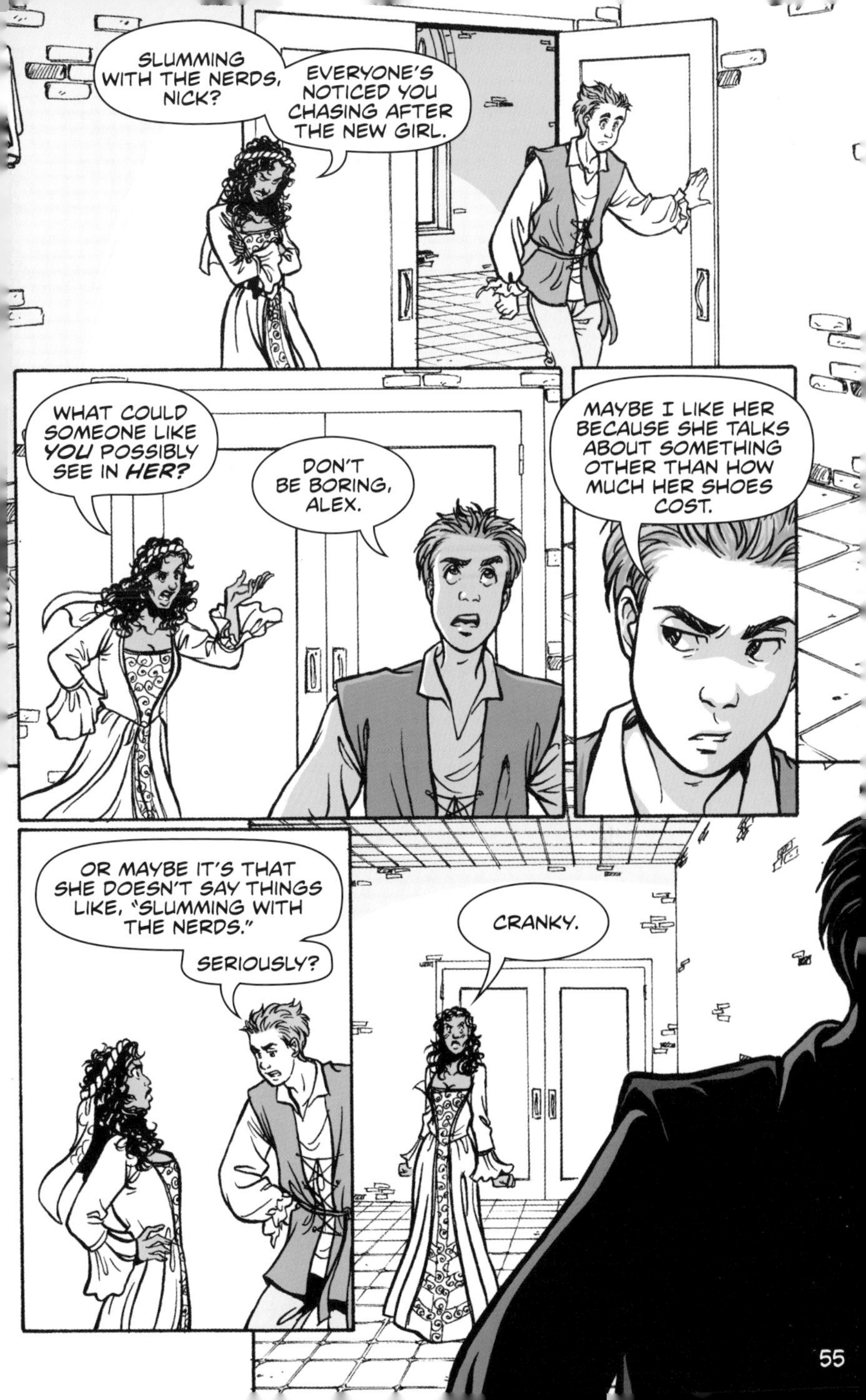
SLUMMING WITH THE NERDS, NICK?
EVERYONE'S NOTICED YOU CHASING AFTER THE NEW GIRL.
WHAT COULD SOMEONE LIKE *YOU* POSSIBLY SEE IN *HER*?
DON'T BE BORING, ALEX.
MAYBE I LIKE HER BECAUSE SHE TALKS ABOUT SOMETHING OTHER THAN HOW MUCH HER SHOES COST.
OR MAYBE IT'S THAT SHE DOESN'T SAY THINGS LIKE, "SLUMMING WITH THE NERDS."
SERIOUSLY?
CRANKY.

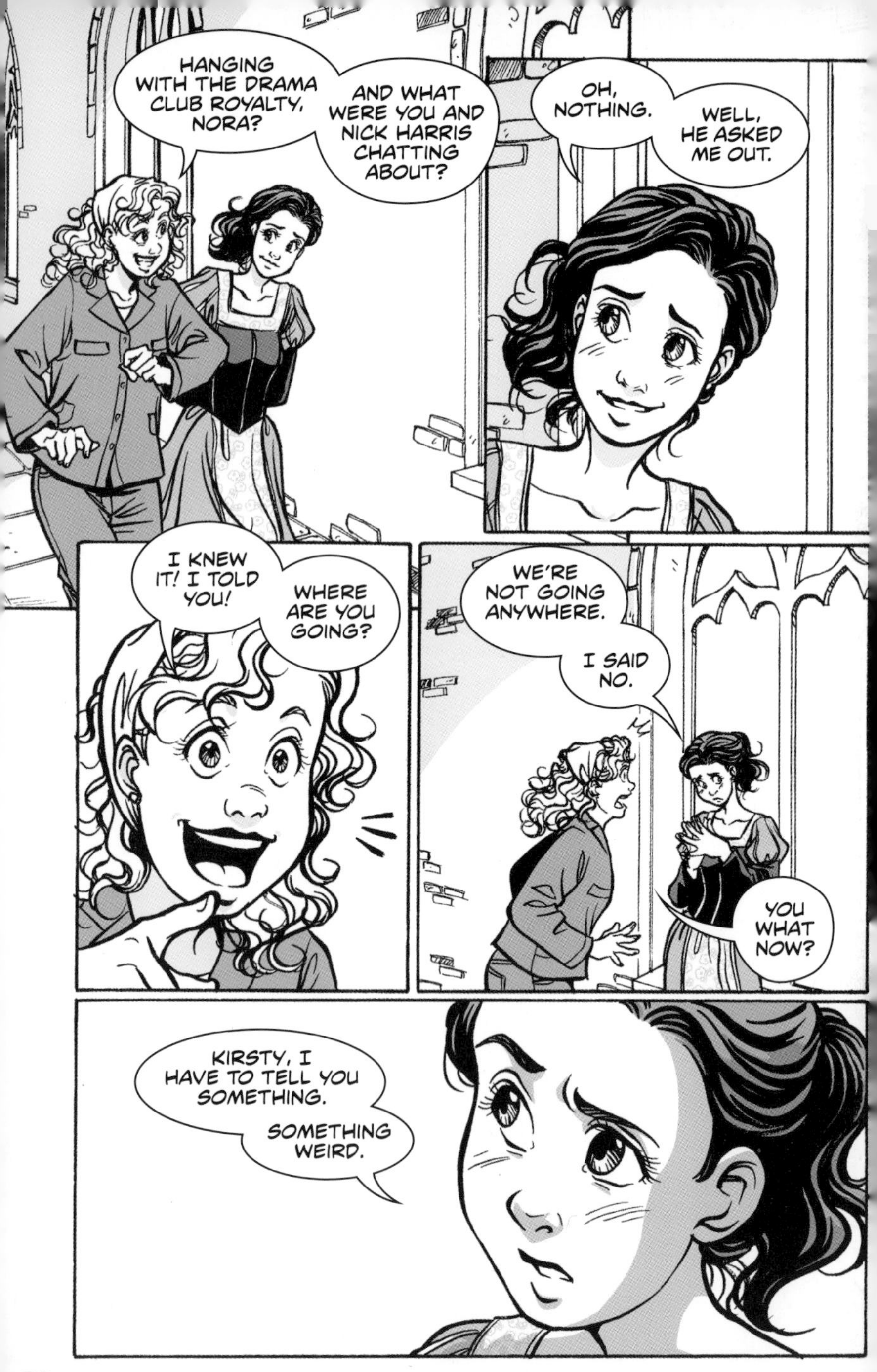

HANGING WITH THE DRAMA CLUB ROYALTY, NORA?
AND WHAT WERE YOU AND NICK HARRIS CHATTING ABOUT?
OH, NOTHING.
WELL, HE ASKED ME OUT.
I KNEW IT! I TOLD YOU!
WHERE ARE YOU GOING?
WE'RE NOT GOING ANYWHERE.
I SAID NO.
YOU WHAT NOW?
KIRSTY, I HAVE TO TELL YOU SOMETHING.
SOMETHING WEIRD.

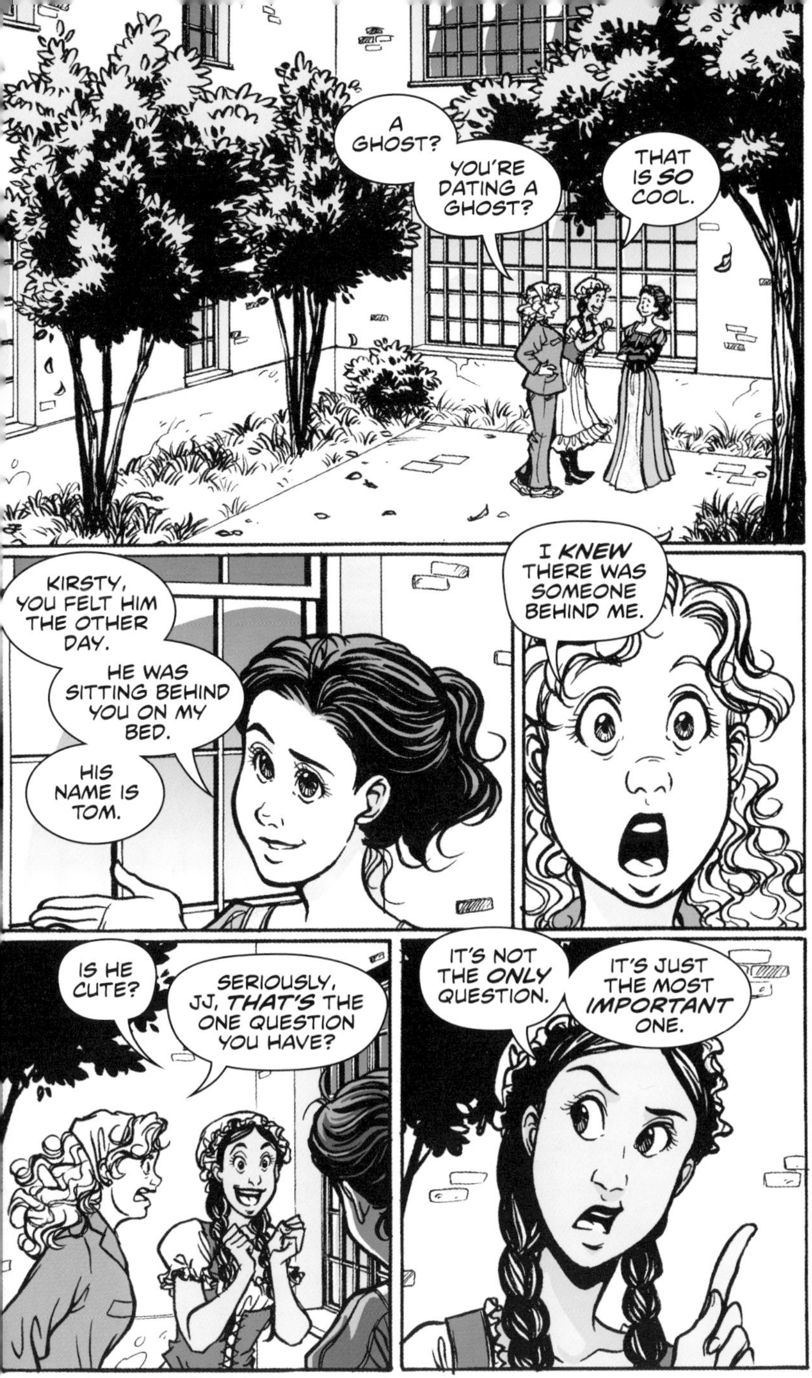
A GHOST?
YOU'RE DATING A GHOST?
THAT IS *SO* COOL.
KIRSTY, YOU FELT HIM THE OTHER DAY.
HE WAS SITTING BEHIND YOU ON MY BED.
HIS NAME IS TOM.
I *KNEW* THERE WAS SOMEONE BEHIND ME.
IS HE CUTE?
SERIOUSLY, JJ, *THAT'S* THE ONE QUESTION YOU HAVE?
IT'S NOT THE *ONLY* QUESTION.
IT'S JUST THE MOST *IMPORTANT* ONE.

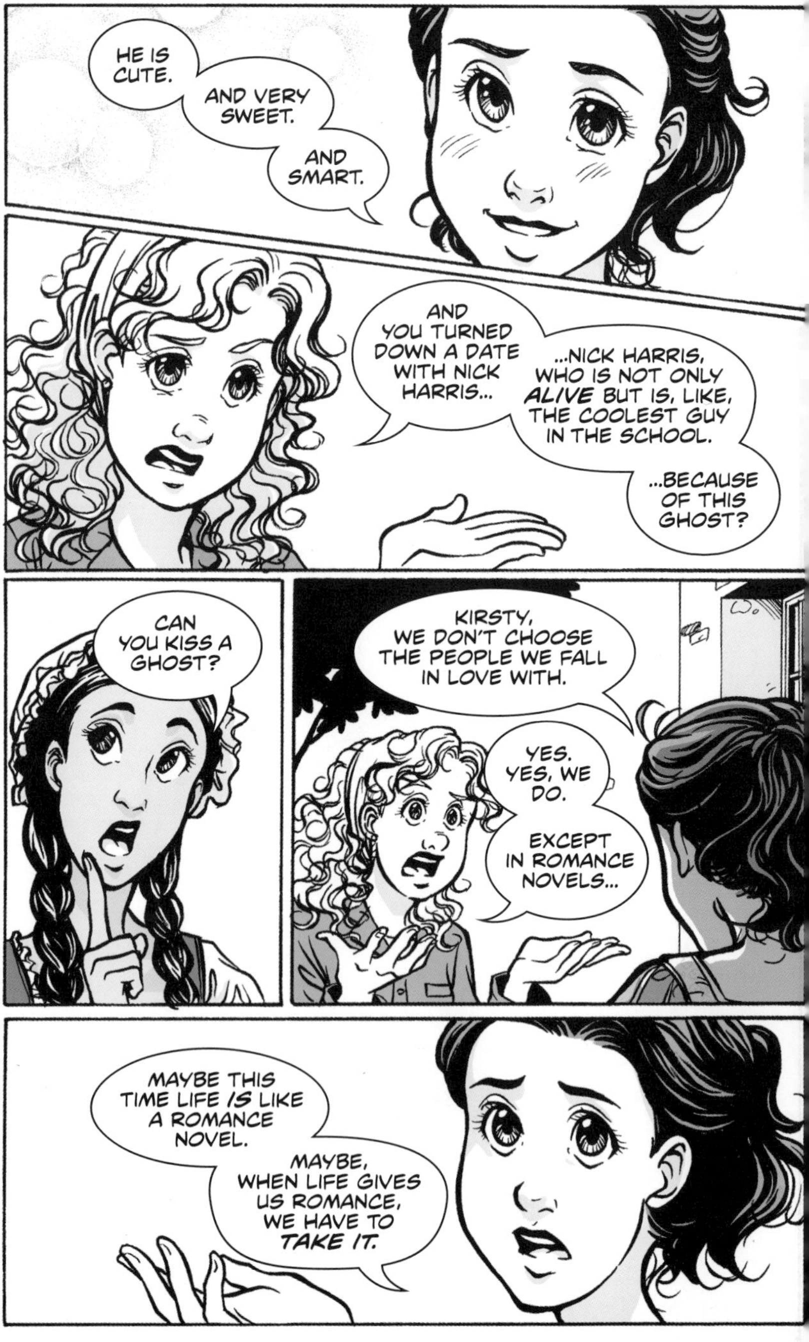
HE IS CUTE.
AND VERY SWEET.
AND SMART.
AND YOU TURNED DOWN A DATE WITH NICK HARRIS...
...NICK HARRIS, WHO IS NOT ONLY *ALIVE* BUT IS, LIKE, THE COOLEST GUY IN THE SCHOOL.
...BECAUSE OF THIS GHOST?
CAN YOU KISS A GHOST?
KIRSTY, WE DON'T CHOOSE THE PEOPLE WE FALL IN LOVE WITH.
YES. YES, WE DO.
EXCEPT IN ROMANCE NOVELS...
MAYBE THIS TIME LIFE *IS* LIKE A ROMANCE NOVEL.
MAYBE, WHEN LIFE GIVES US ROMANCE, WE HAVE TO *TAKE IT.*

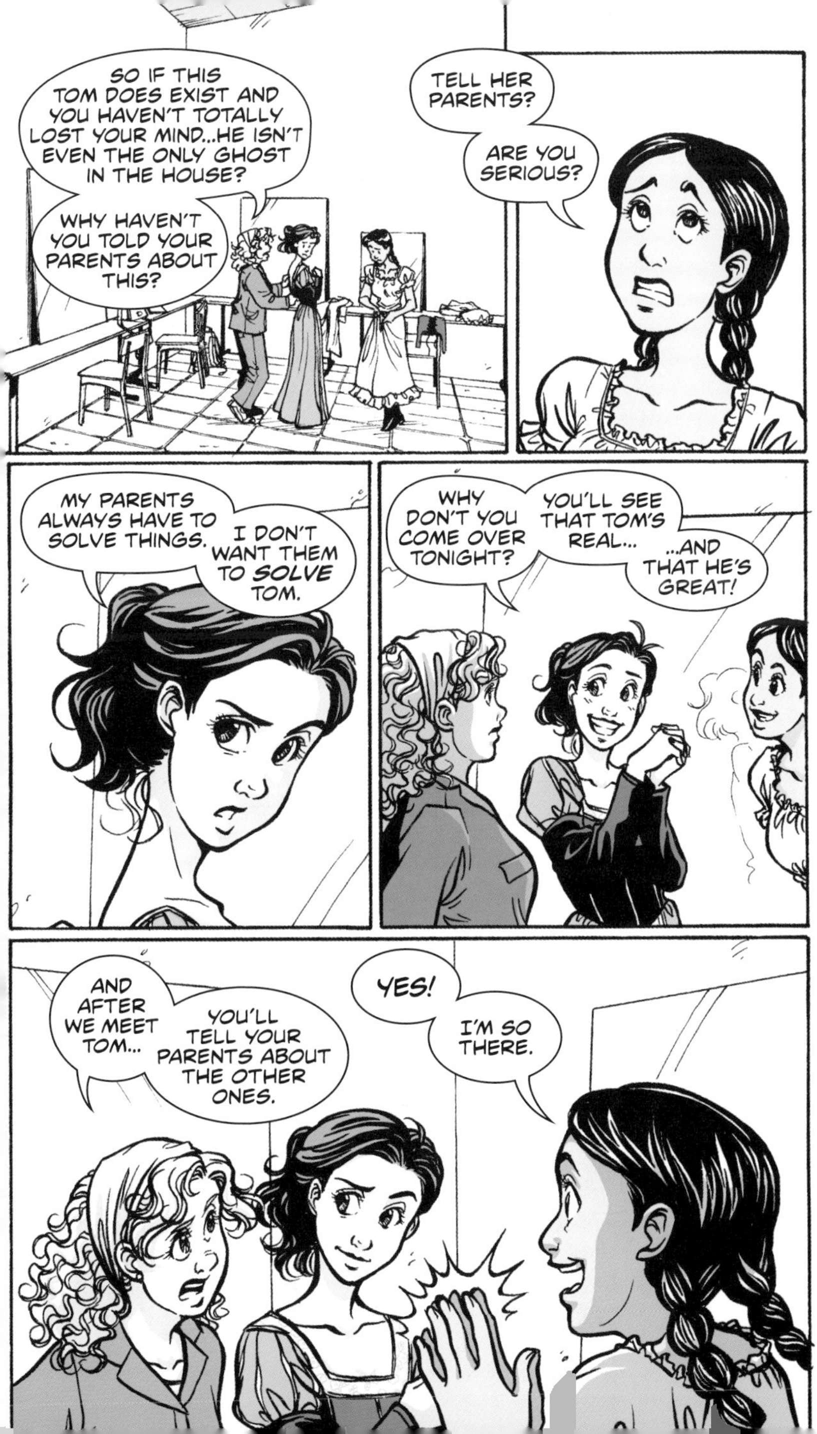
SO IF THIS TOM DOES EXIST AND YOU HAVEN'T TOTALLY LOST YOUR MIND...HE ISN'T EVEN THE ONLY GHOST IN THE HOUSE?
WHY HAVEN'T YOU TOLD YOUR PARENTS ABOUT THIS?
TELL HER PARENTS?
ARE YOU SERIOUS?
MY PARENTS ALWAYS HAVE TO SOLVE THINGS.
I DON'T WANT THEM TO *SOLVE* TOM.
WHY DON'T YOU COME OVER TONIGHT?
YOU'LL SEE THAT TOM'S REAL...
...AND THAT HE'S GREAT!
AND AFTER WE MEET TOM...
YOU'LL TELL YOUR PARENTS ABOUT THE OTHER ONES.
YES!
I'M SO THERE.

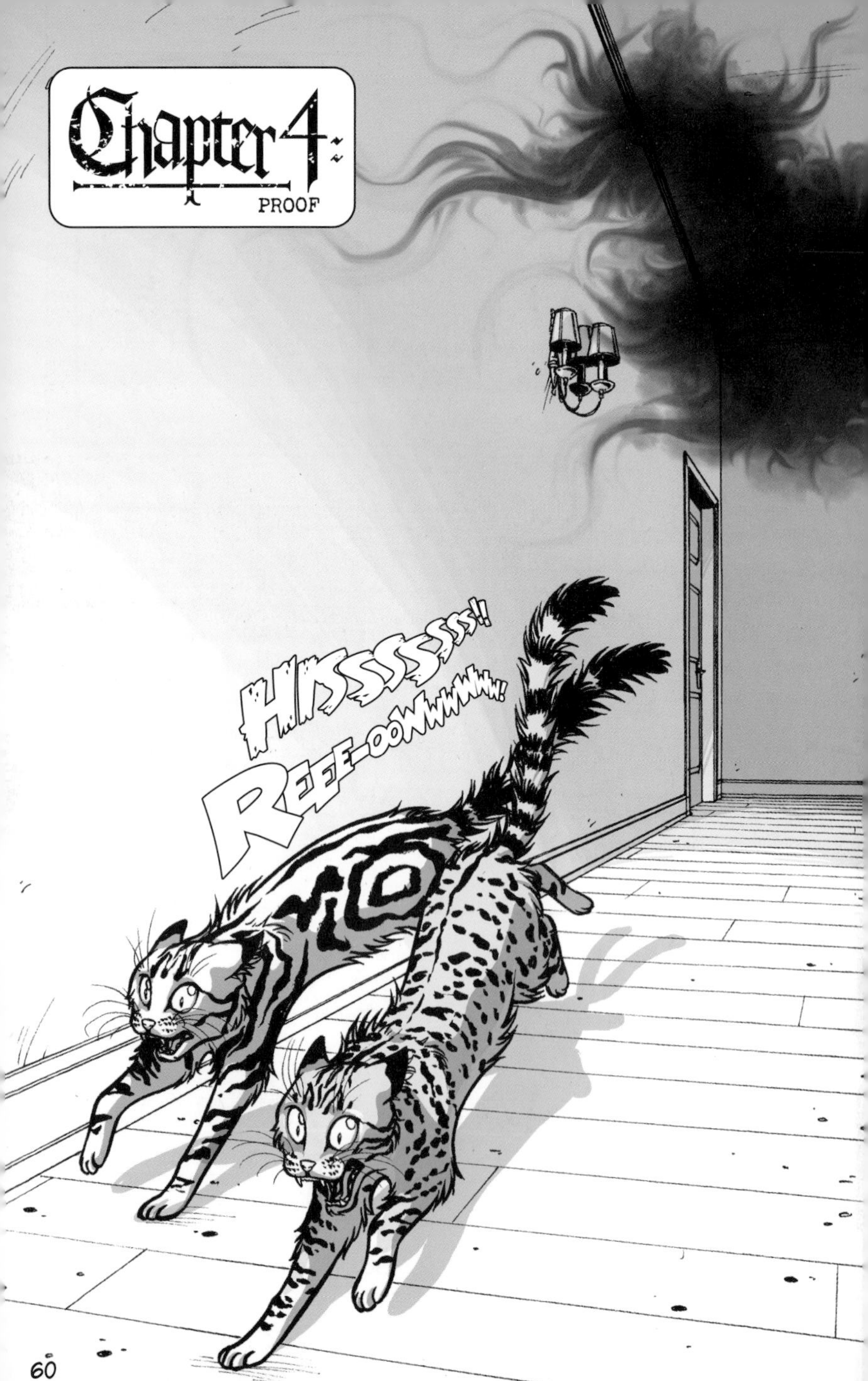
Chapter 4:
PROOF
HISSSSSSS!!
REEE-OONWWWWW!

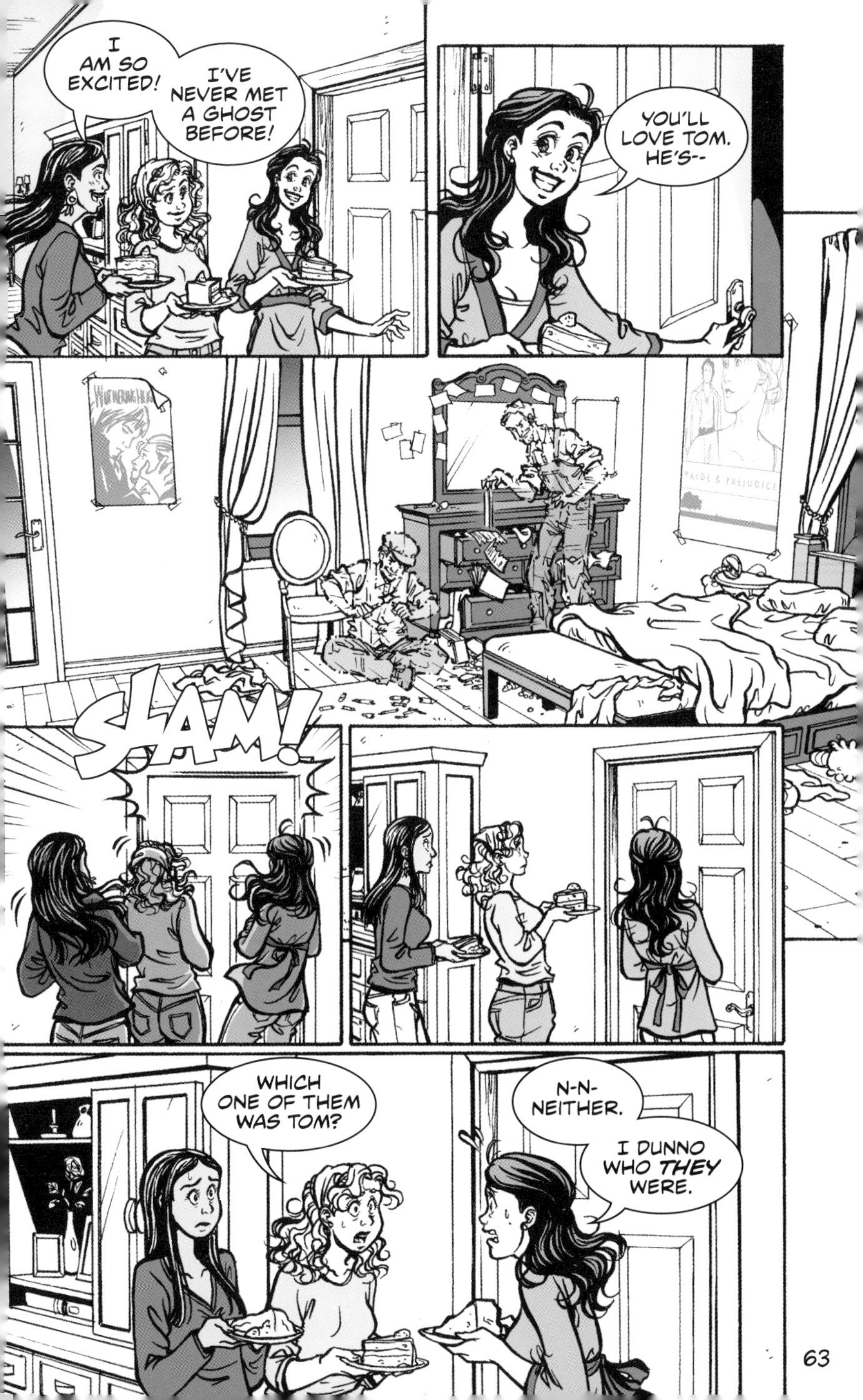
I AM SO EXCITED!
I'VE NEVER MET A GHOST BEFORE!
YOU'LL LOVE TOM. HE'S--
WUTHERING HEIGHTS
PRIDE & PREJUDICE
SLAM!
WHICH ONE OF THEM WAS TOM?
N-N-NEITHER.
I DUNNO WHO *THEY* WERE.

64

69

71

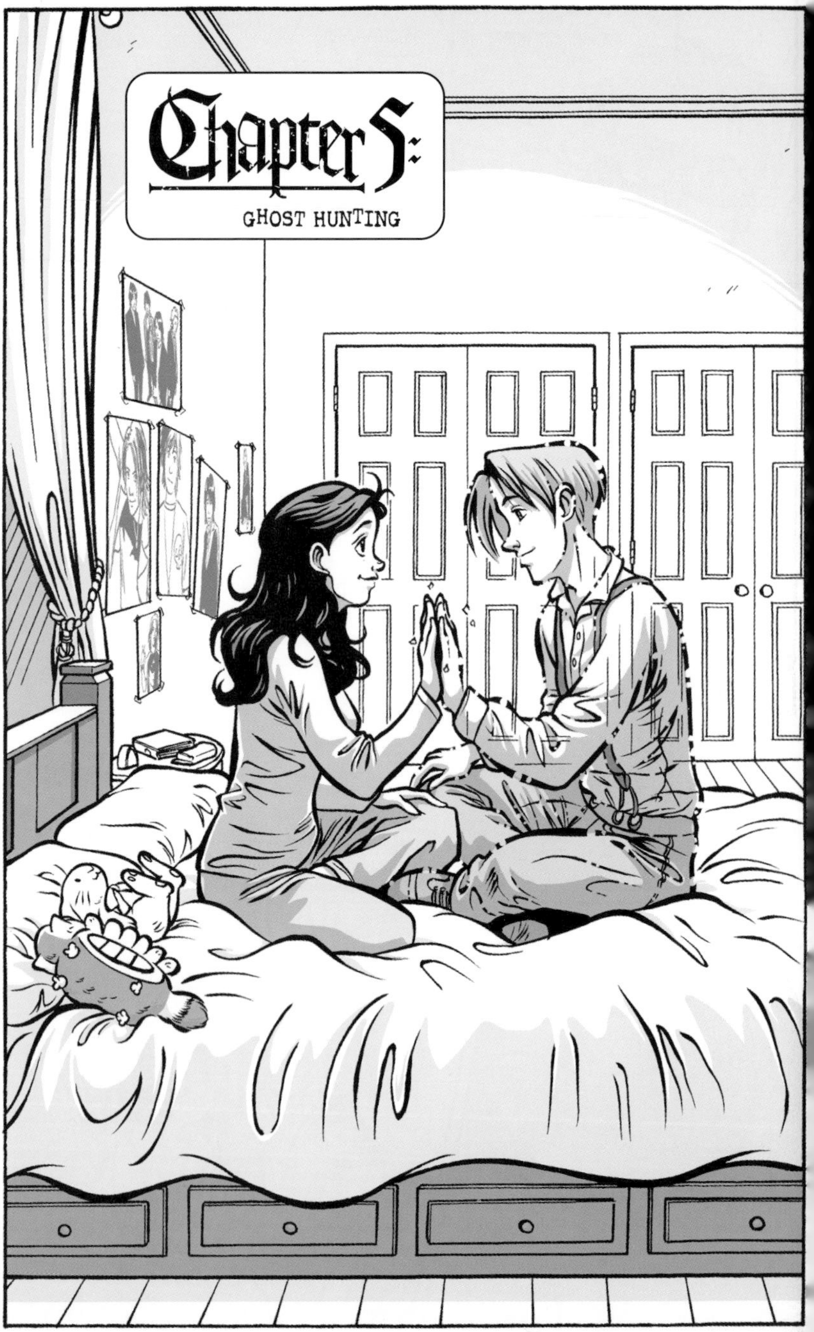
Chapter 5:
GHOST HUNTING

75

78

WE'RE GOING TO TRY ONE MORE THING BEFORE WE LEAVE.

IT'S AN OLD TRICK.

I'M GOING TO THROW THIS BALL DOWN THE HALLWAY...

...AND HOPE THAT ONE OF THE GHOSTS THROWS IT BACK.

NOTHING.

ALL RIGHT.

I'LL GO GET THE BALL.

I HEARD IT STOP BOUNCING.

WHERE IS IT?

83

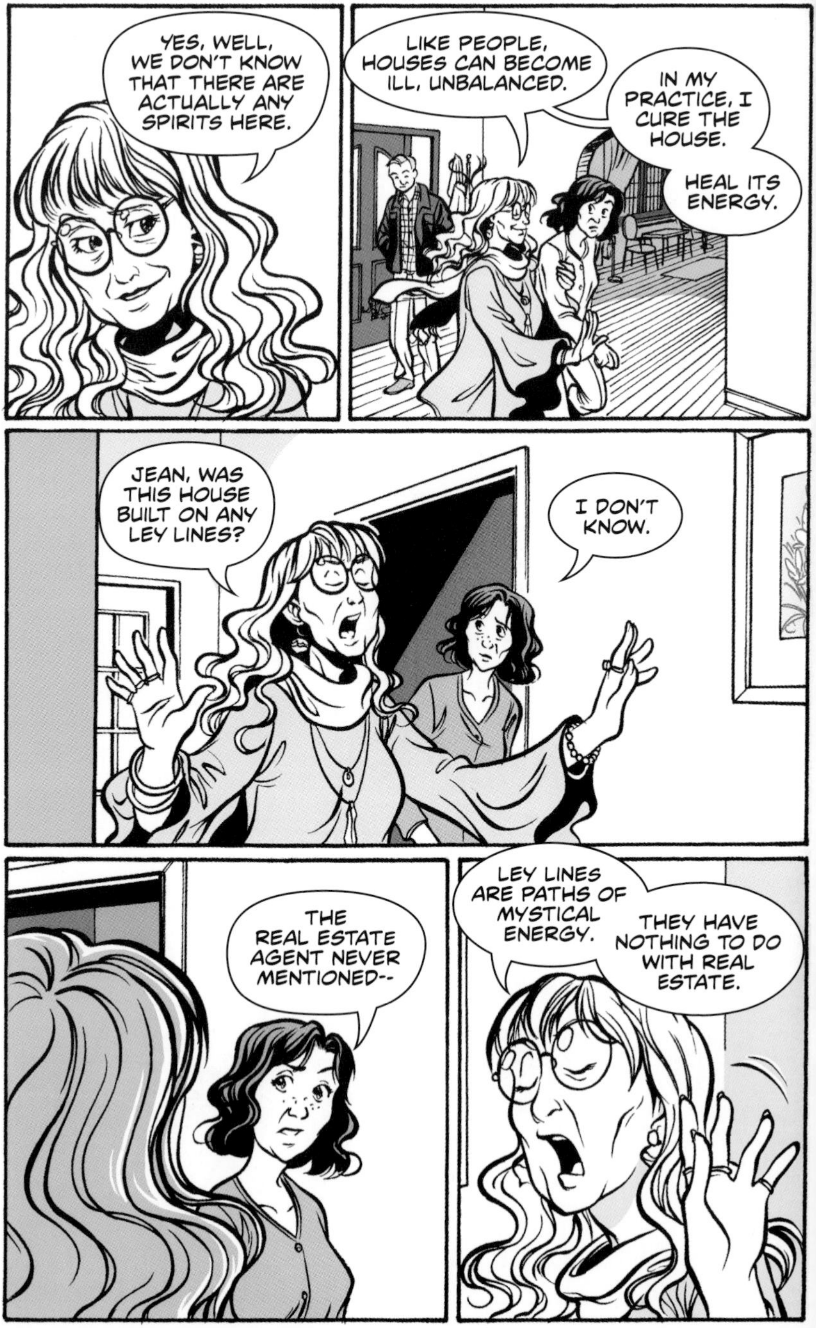
YES, WELL, WE DON'T KNOW THAT THERE ARE ACTUALLY ANY SPIRITS HERE.
LIKE PEOPLE, HOUSES CAN BECOME ILL, UNBALANCED.
IN MY PRACTICE, I CURE THE HOUSE.
HEAL ITS ENERGY.
JEAN, WAS THIS HOUSE BUILT ON ANY LEY LINES?
I DON'T KNOW.
THE REAL ESTATE AGENT NEVER MENTIONED--
LEY LINES ARE PATHS OF MYSTICAL ENERGY.
THEY HAVE NOTHING TO DO WITH REAL ESTATE.

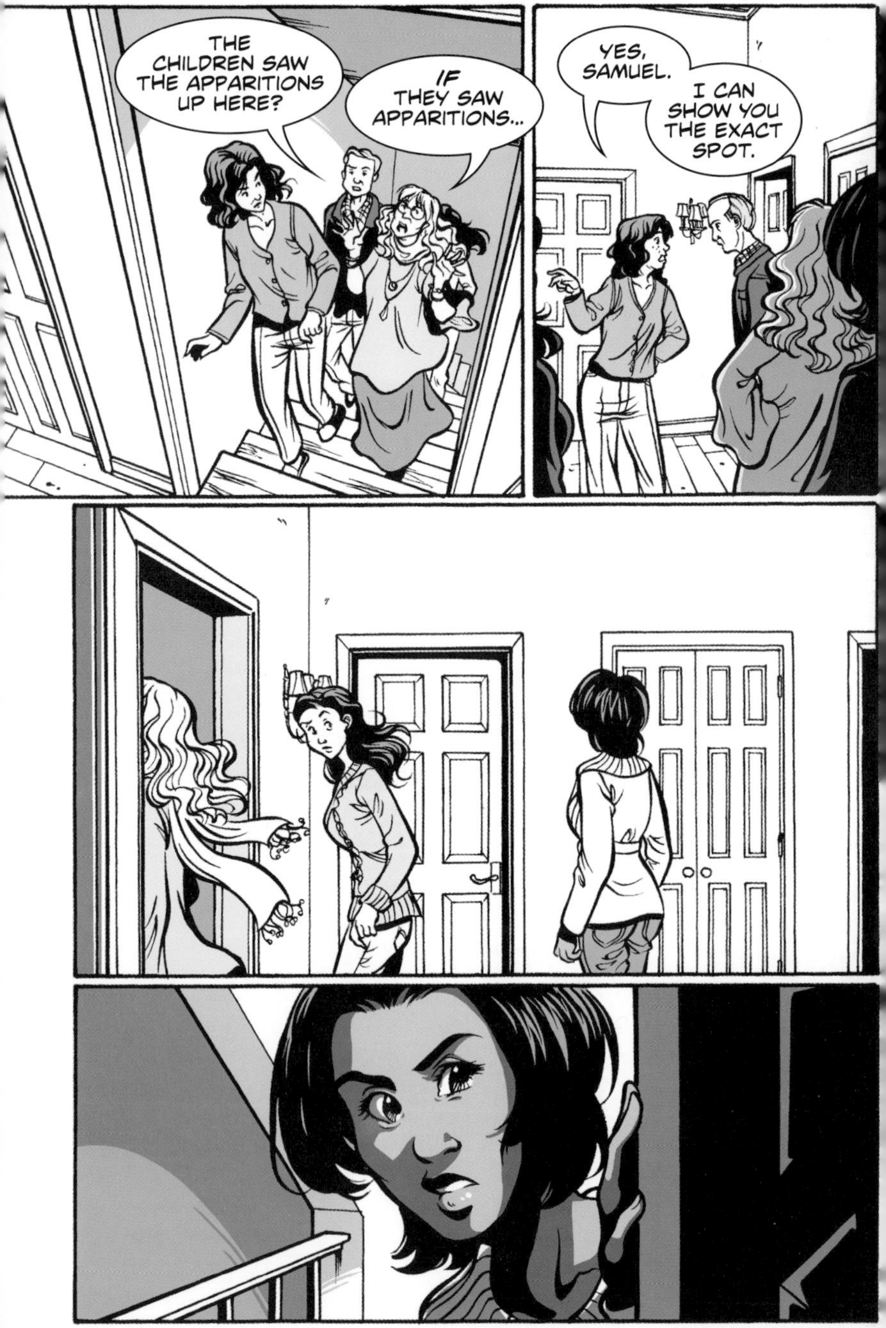
THE CHILDREN SAW THE APPARITIONS UP HERE?
IF THEY SAW APPARITIONS...
YES, SAMUEL.
I CAN SHOW YOU THE EXACT SPOT.

89

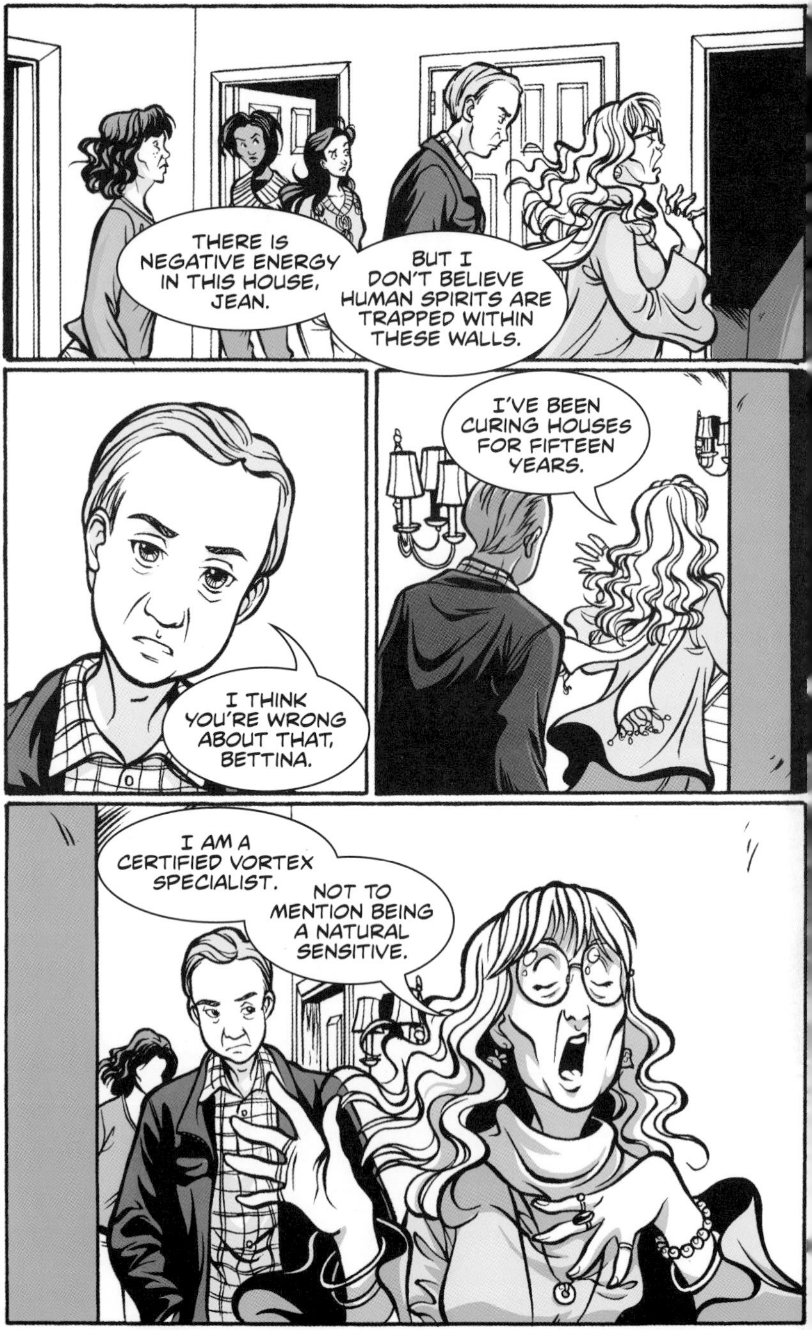
THERE IS NEGATIVE ENERGY IN THIS HOUSE, JEAN.
BUT I DON'T BELIEVE HUMAN SPIRITS ARE TRAPPED WITHIN THESE WALLS.
I THINK YOU'RE WRONG ABOUT THAT, BETTINA.
I'VE BEEN CURING HOUSES FOR FIFTEEN YEARS.
I AM A CERTIFIED VORTEX SPECIALIST.
NOT TO MENTION BEING A NATURAL SENSITIVE.

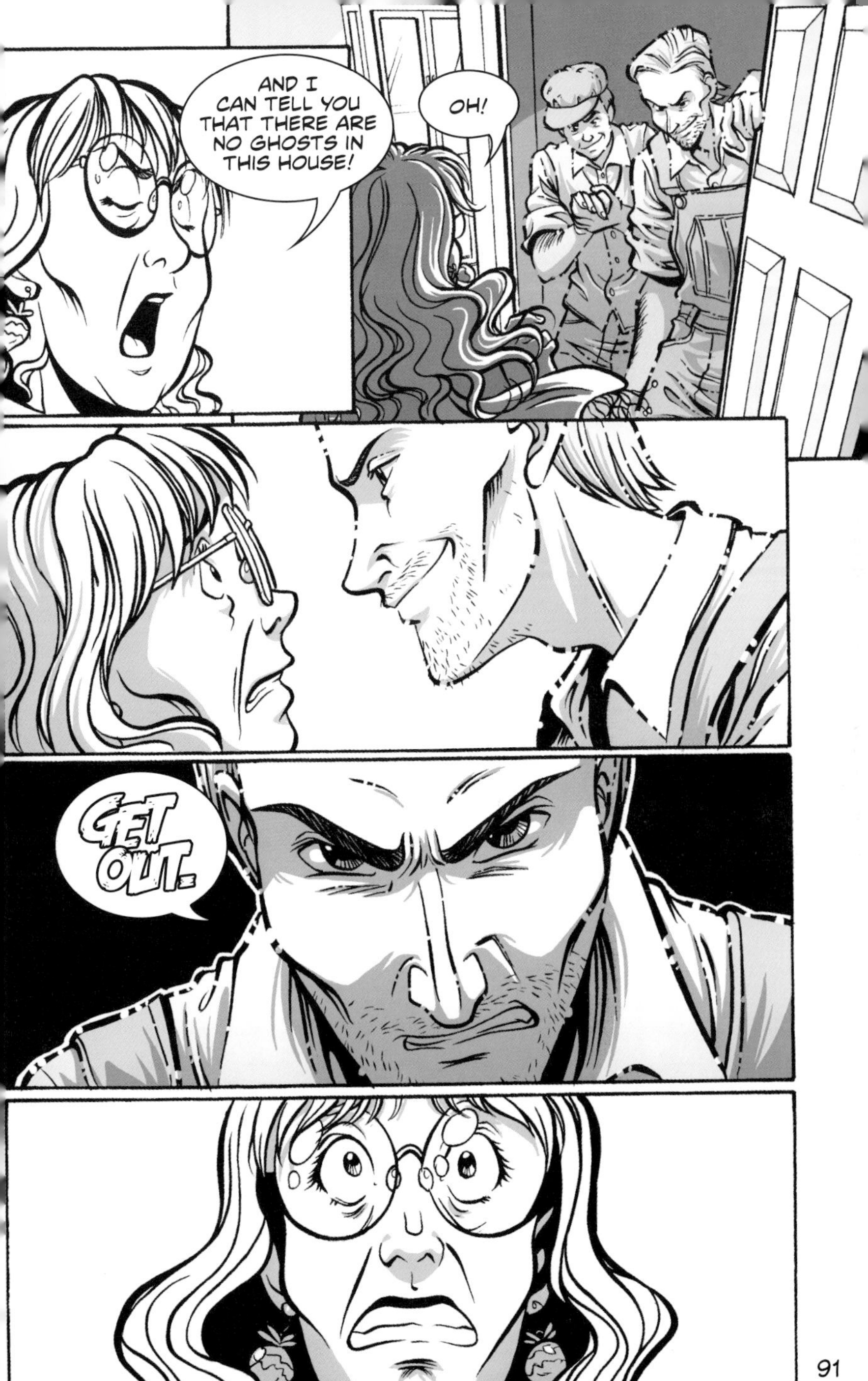
AND I CAN TELL YOU THAT THERE ARE NO GHOSTS IN THIS HOUSE!
OH!
GET OUT.

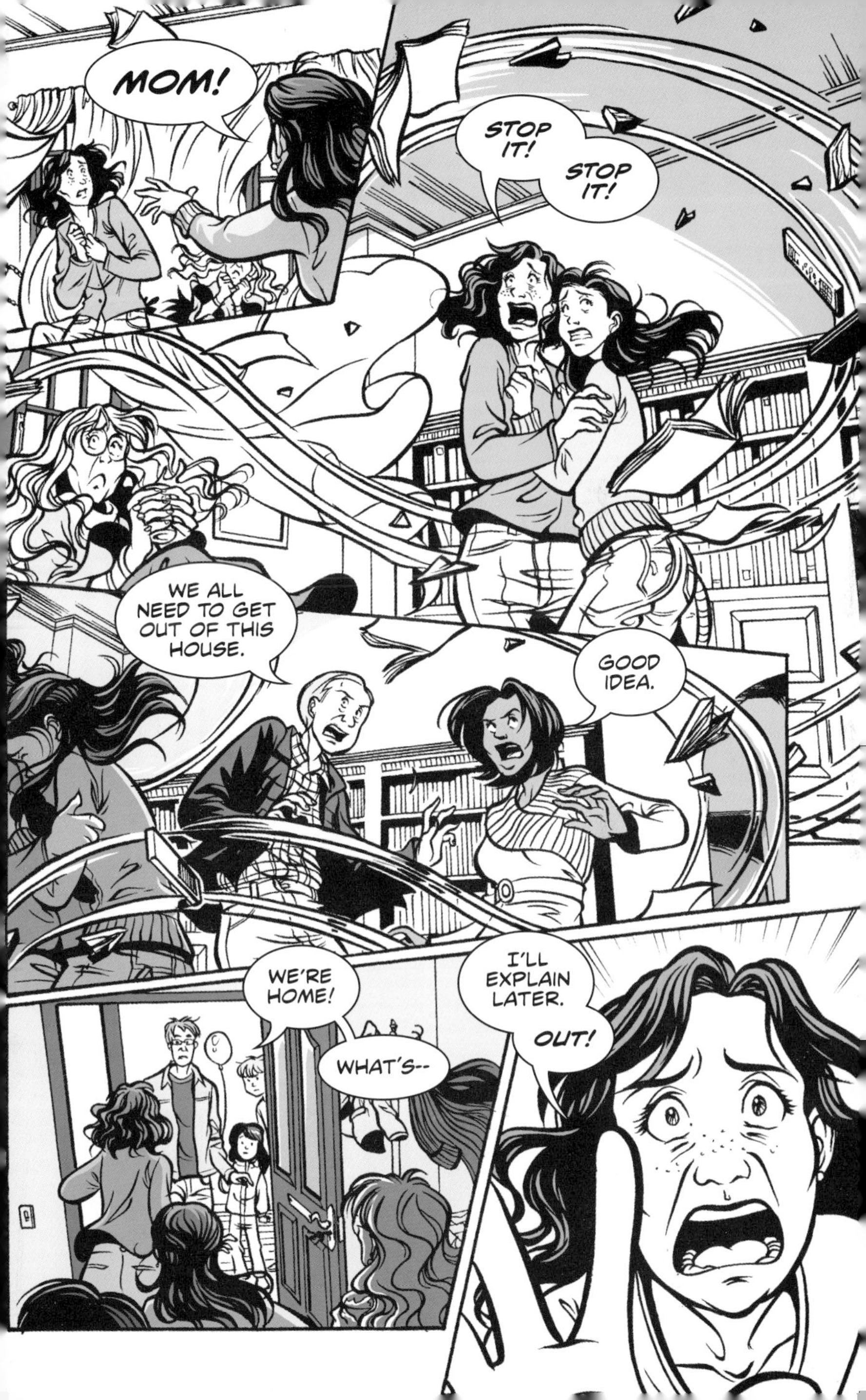
MOM!
STOP IT!
STOP IT!
WE ALL NEED TO GET OUT OF THIS HOUSE.
GOOD IDEA.
WE'RE HOME!
WHAT'S--
I'LL EXPLAIN LATER.
OUT!

Chapter 6:
CROSSING OVER

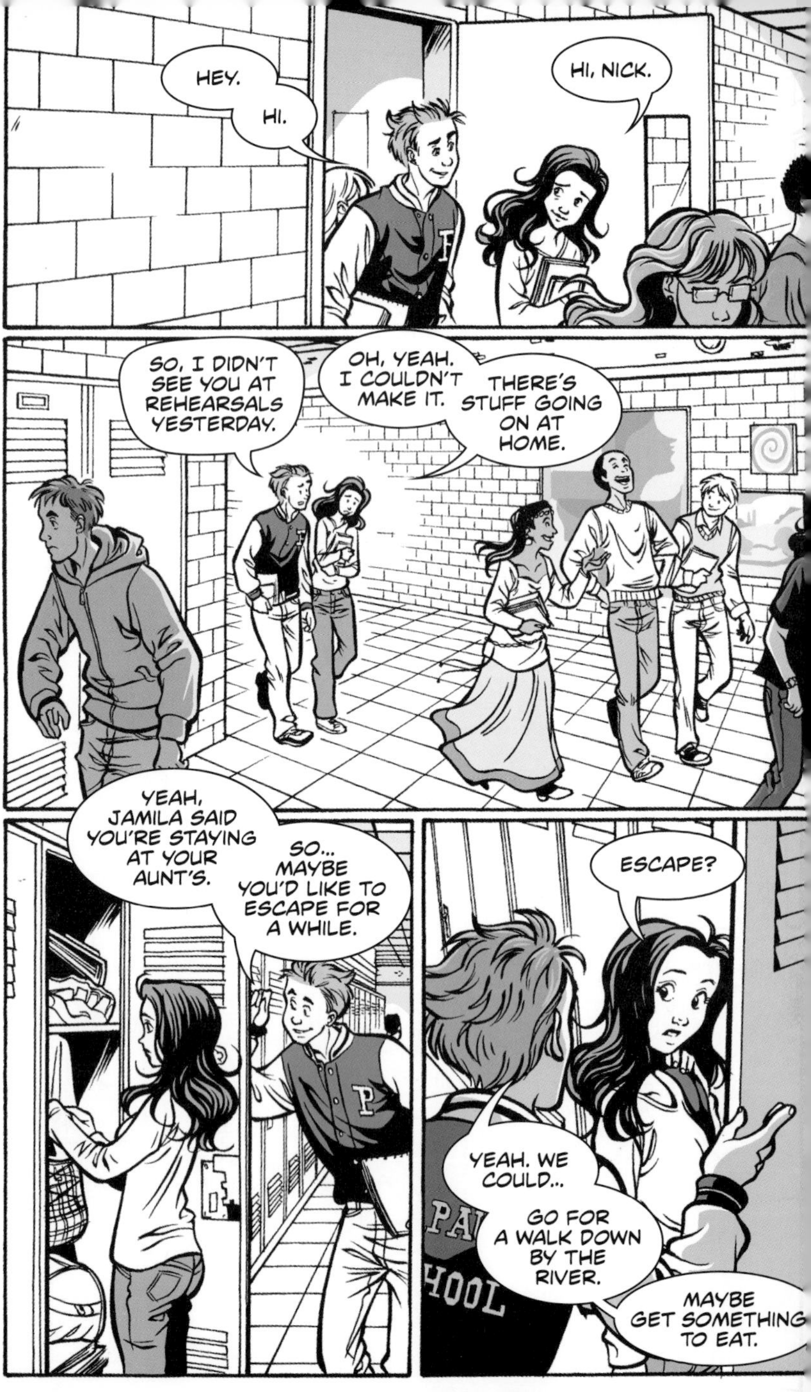
HEY.
HI.
HI, NICK.
SO, I DIDN'T SEE YOU AT REHEARSALS YESTERDAY.
OH, YEAH. I COULDN'T MAKE IT.
THERE'S STUFF GOING ON AT HOME.
YEAH, JAMILA SAID YOU'RE STAYING AT YOUR AUNT'S.
SO... MAYBE YOU'D LIKE TO ESCAPE FOR A WHILE.
ESCAPE?
YEAH. WE COULD...
GO FOR A WALK DOWN BY THE RIVER.
MAYBE GET SOMETHING TO EAT.

97

Archer Corporation

Katherine Hill
Senior Technical Writer

If you need anything, call me at
home: 651-555-6709

Two Down Coffee Shop
356 Third Street

THERE YOU ARE!

LET'S GO IN.

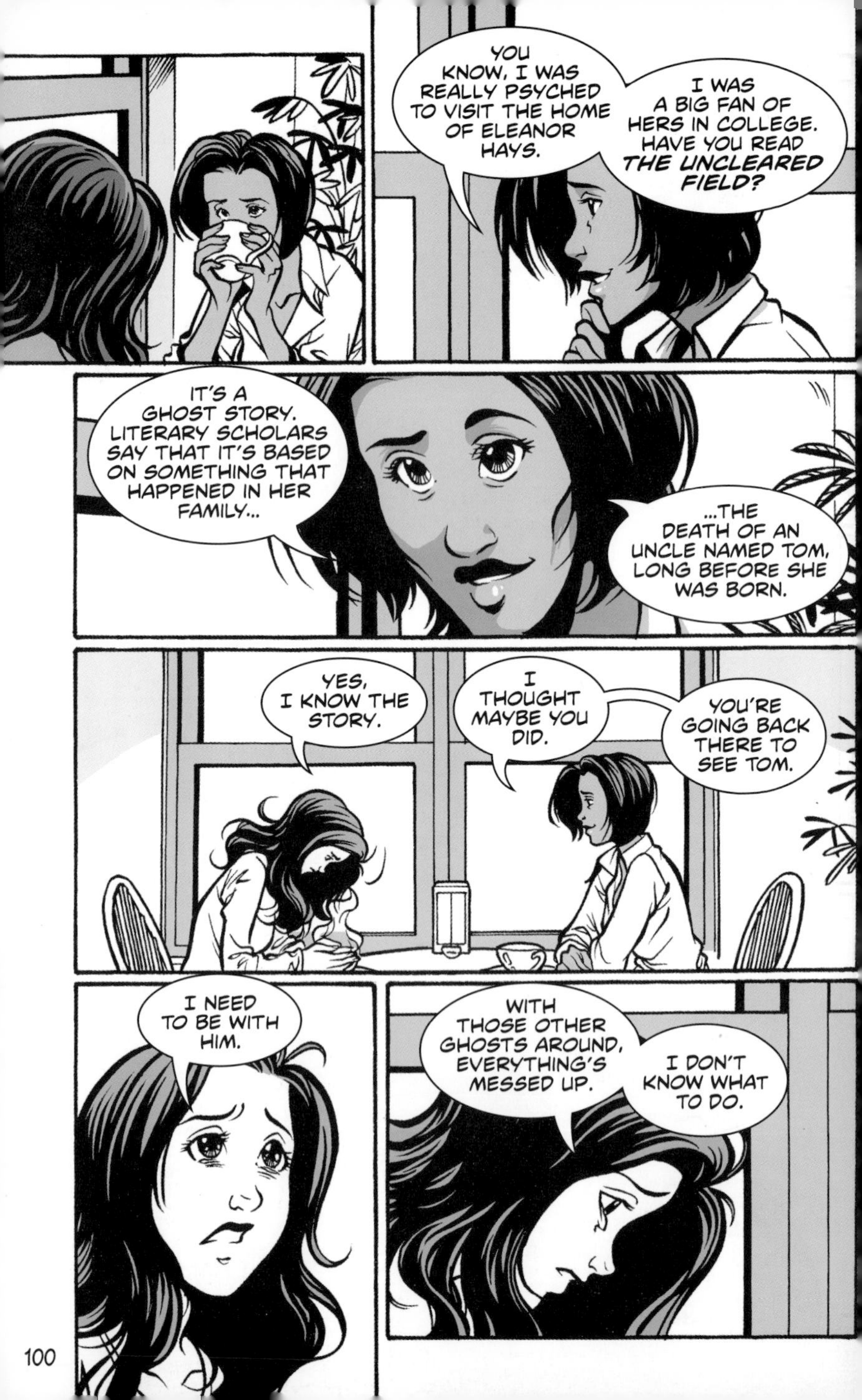
YOU KNOW, I WAS REALLY PSYCHED TO VISIT THE HOME OF ELEANOR HAYS.
I WAS A BIG FAN OF HERS IN COLLEGE. HAVE YOU READ *THE UNCLEARED FIELD?*
IT'S A GHOST STORY. LITERARY SCHOLARS SAY THAT IT'S BASED ON SOMETHING THAT HAPPENED IN HER FAMILY...
...THE DEATH OF AN UNCLE NAMED TOM, LONG BEFORE SHE WAS BORN.
YES, I KNOW THE STORY.
I THOUGHT MAYBE YOU DID.
YOU'RE GOING BACK THERE TO SEE TOM.
I NEED TO BE WITH HIM.
WITH THOSE OTHER GHOSTS AROUND, EVERYTHING'S MESSED UP.
I DON'T KNOW WHAT TO DO.

101

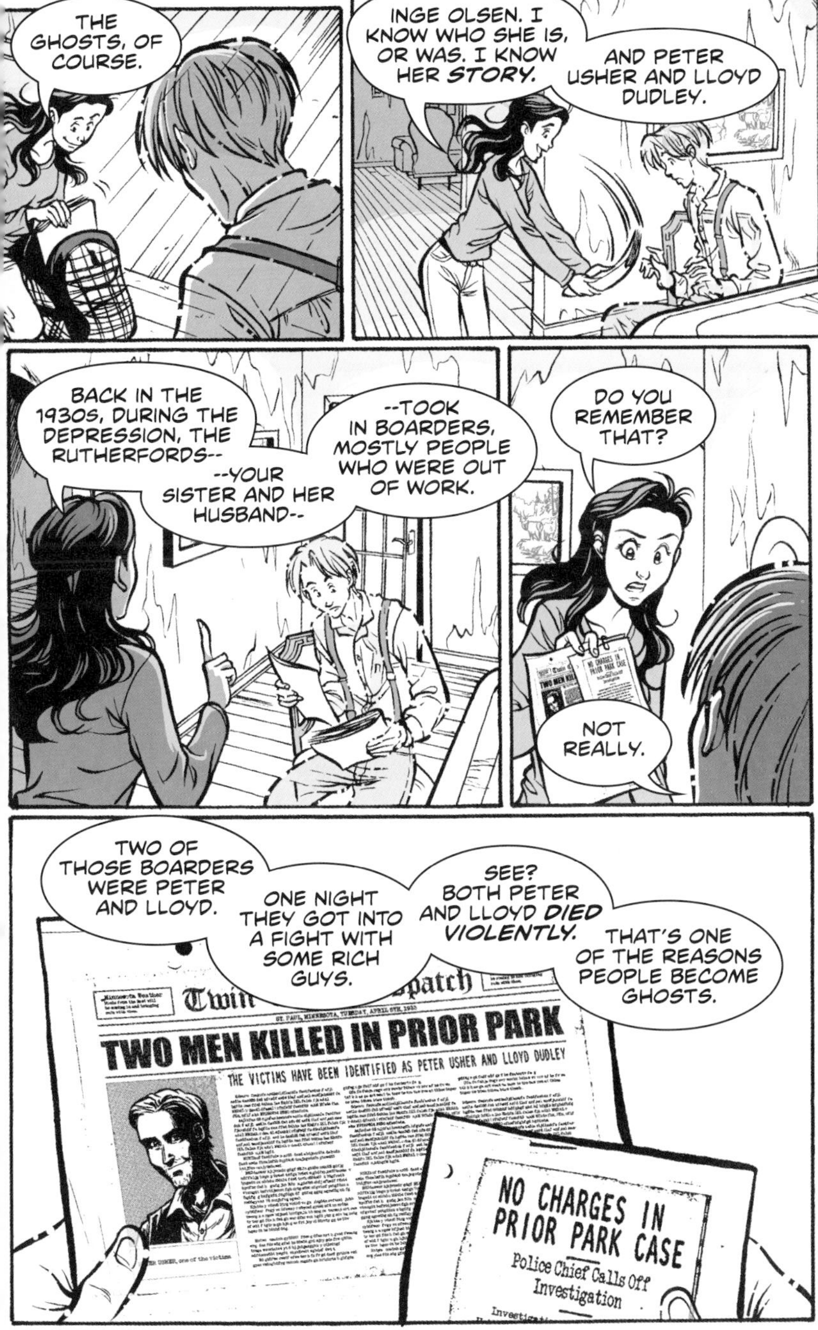
THE GHOSTS, OF COURSE.
INGE OLSEN. I KNOW WHO SHE IS, OR WAS. I KNOW HER *STORY.*
AND PETER USHER AND LLOYD DUDLEY.
BACK IN THE 1930S, DURING THE DEPRESSION, THE RUTHERFORDS--
--YOUR SISTER AND HER HUSBAND--
--TOOK IN BOARDERS, MOSTLY PEOPLE WHO WERE OUT OF WORK.
DO YOU REMEMBER THAT?
NOT REALLY.
TWO OF THOSE BOARDERS WERE PETER AND LLOYD.
ONE NIGHT THEY GOT INTO A FIGHT WITH SOME RICH GUYS.
SEE? BOTH PETER AND LLOYD ***DIED VIOLENTLY.***
THAT'S ONE OF THE REASONS PEOPLE BECOME GHOSTS.
TWO MEN KILLED IN PRIOR PARK
THE VICTIMS HAVE BEEN IDENTIFIED AS PETER USHER AND LLOYD DUDLEY
NO CHARGES IN PRIOR PARK CASE
Police Chief Calls Off Investigation

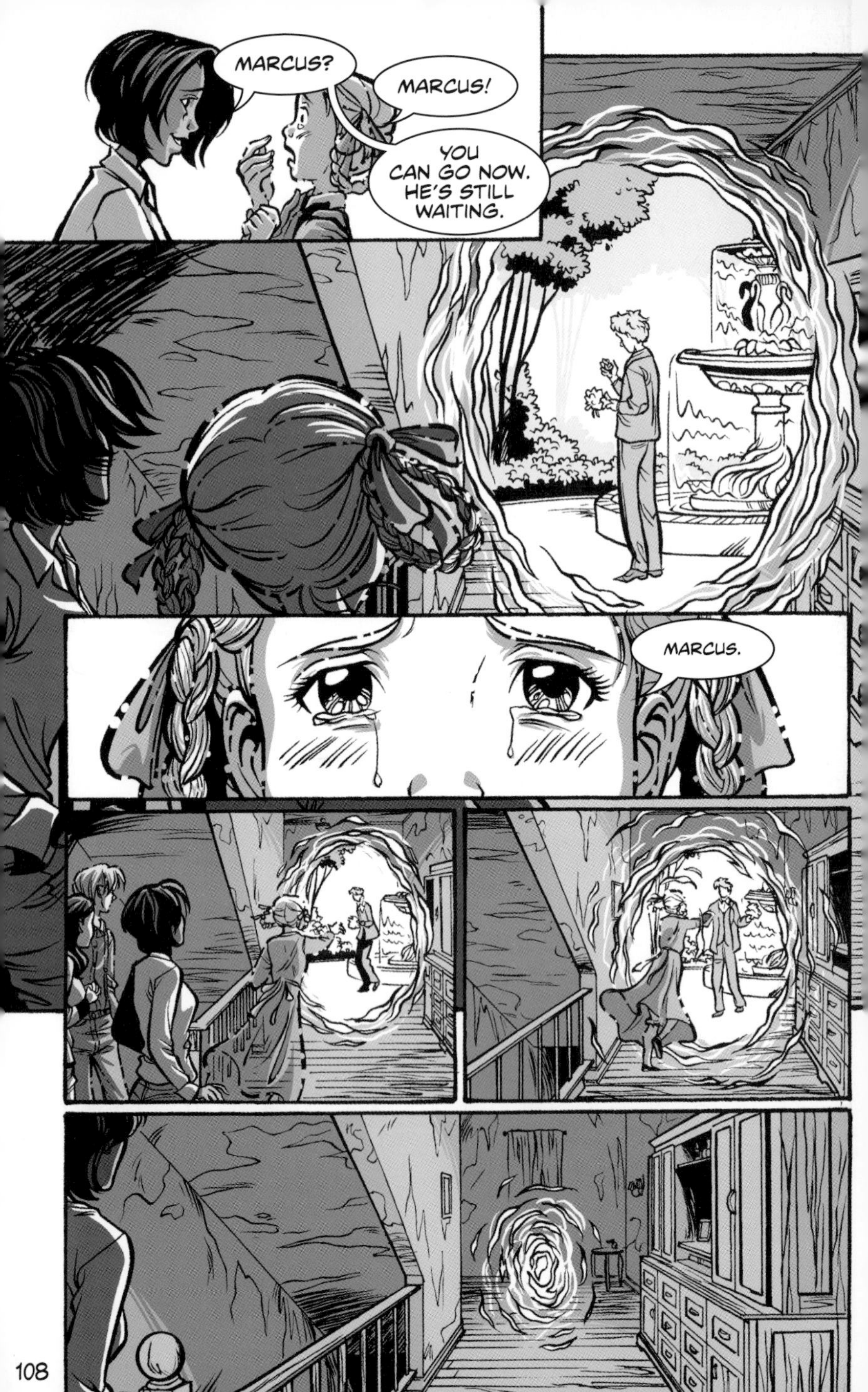
MARCUS?
MARCUS!
YOU CAN GO NOW. HE'S STILL WAITING.
MARCUS.

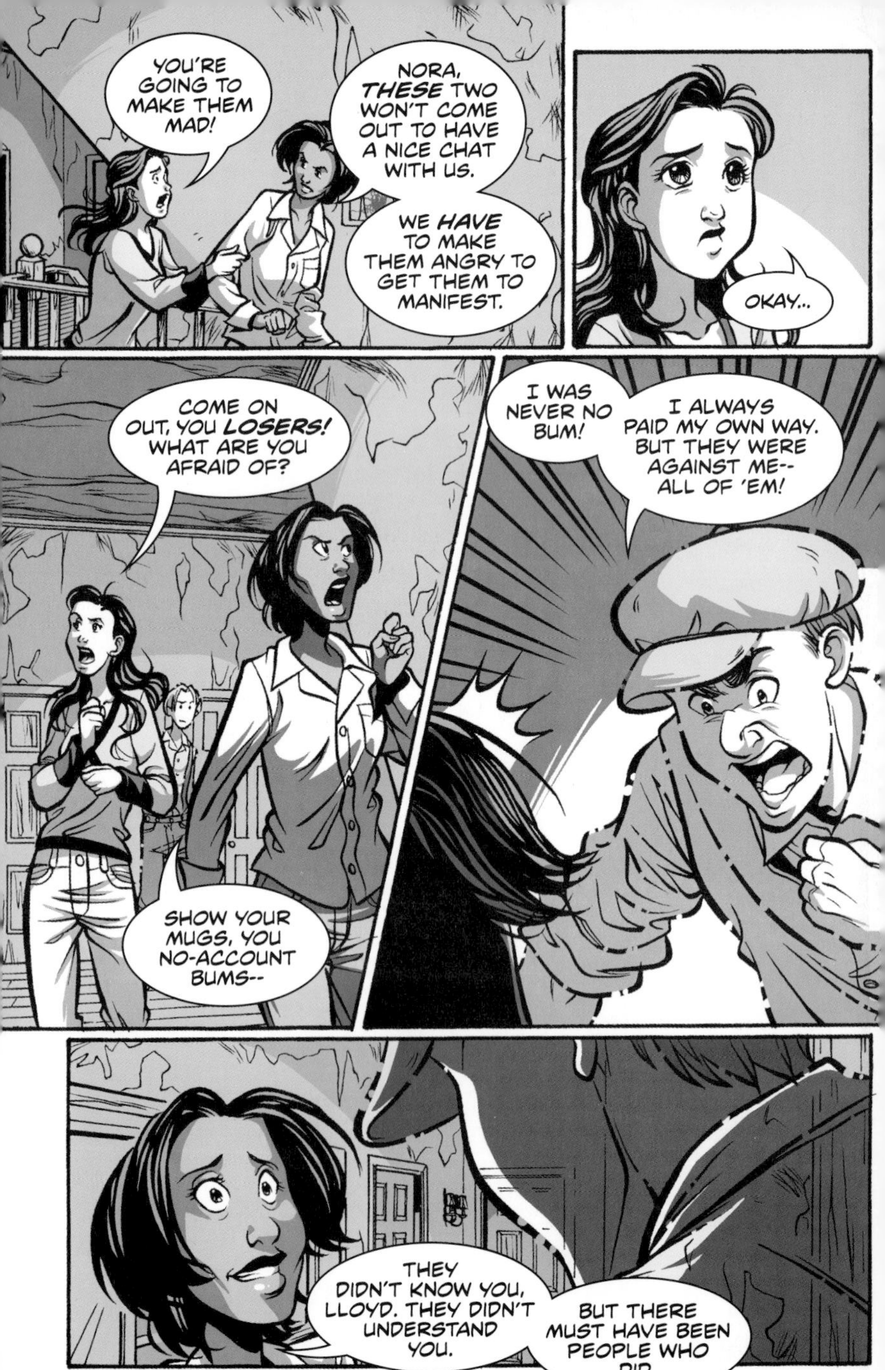
YOU'RE GOING TO MAKE THEM MAD!
NORA, THESE TWO WON'T COME OUT TO HAVE A NICE CHAT WITH US.
WE HAVE TO MAKE THEM ANGRY TO GET THEM TO MANIFEST.
OKAY...
COME ON OUT, YOU LOSERS! WHAT ARE YOU AFRAID OF?
SHOW YOUR MUGS, YOU NO-ACCOUNT BUMS--
I WAS NEVER NO BUM!
I ALWAYS PAID MY OWN WAY. BUT THEY WERE AGAINST ME-- ALL OF 'EM!
THEY DIDN'T KNOW YOU, LLOYD. THEY DIDN'T UNDERSTAND YOU.
BUT THERE MUST HAVE BEEN PEOPLE WHO DID.

113

114

116

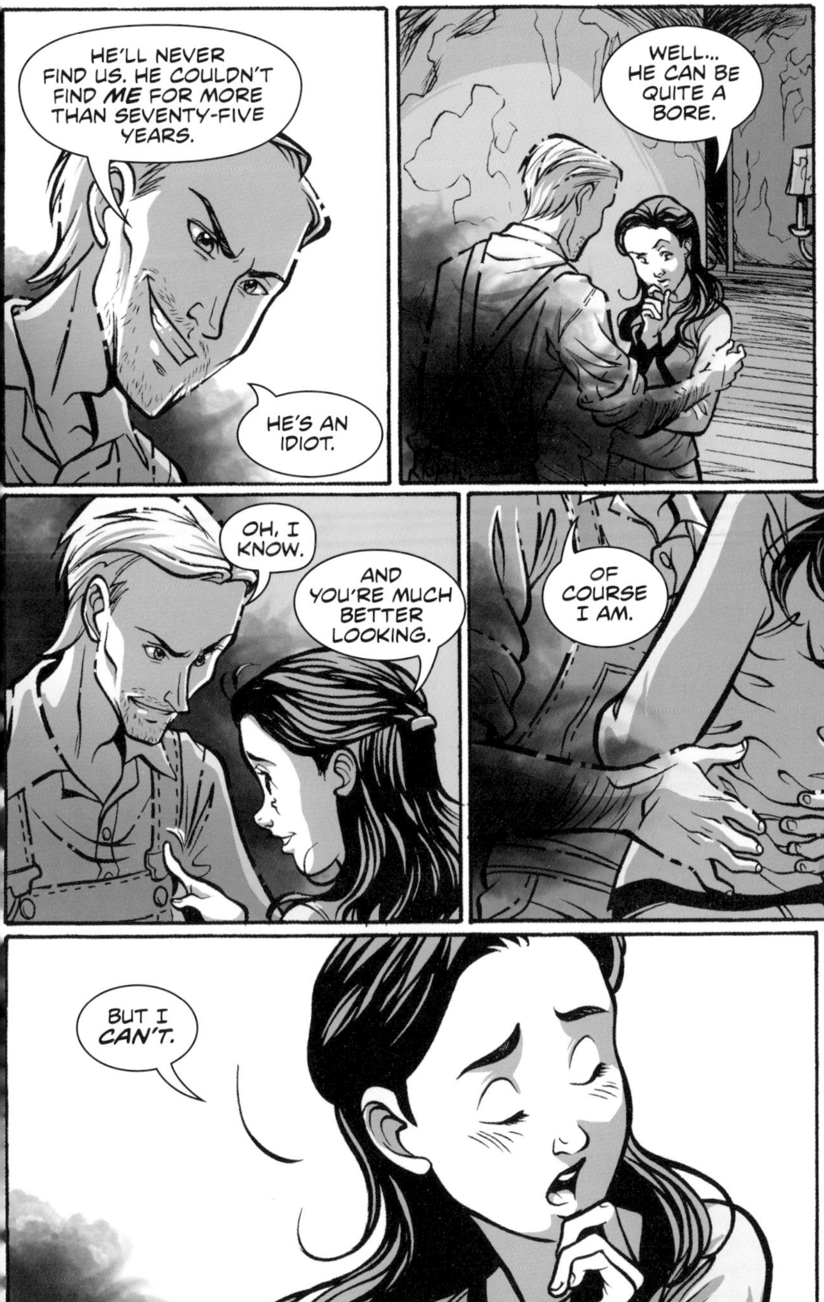
HE'LL NEVER FIND US. HE COULDN'T FIND *ME* FOR MORE THAN SEVENTY-FIVE YEARS.
HE'S AN IDIOT.
WELL... HE CAN BE QUITE A BORE.
OH, I KNOW.
AND YOU'RE MUCH BETTER LOOKING.
OF COURSE I AM.
BUT I *CAN'T*.

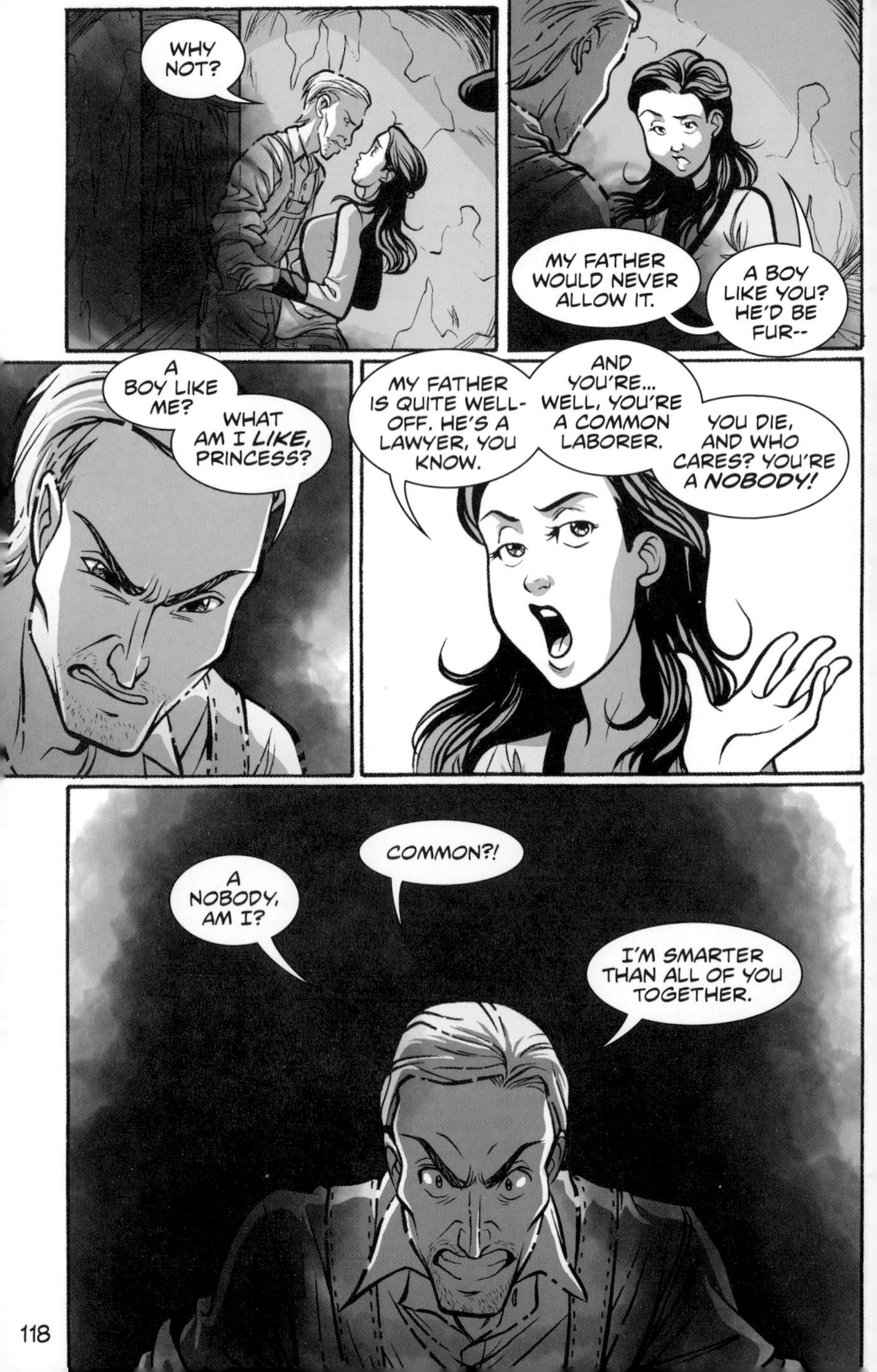
WHY NOT?
MY FATHER WOULD NEVER ALLOW IT.
A BOY LIKE YOU? HE'D BE FUR--
A BOY LIKE ME?
WHAT AM I *LIKE*, PRINCESS?
MY FATHER IS QUITE WELL-OFF. HE'S A LAWYER, YOU KNOW.
AND YOU'RE... WELL, YOU'RE A COMMON LABORER.
YOU DIE, AND WHO CARES? YOU'RE A *NOBODY!*
A NOBODY, AM I?
COMMON?!
I'M SMARTER THAN ALL OF YOU TOGETHER.

119

120

121

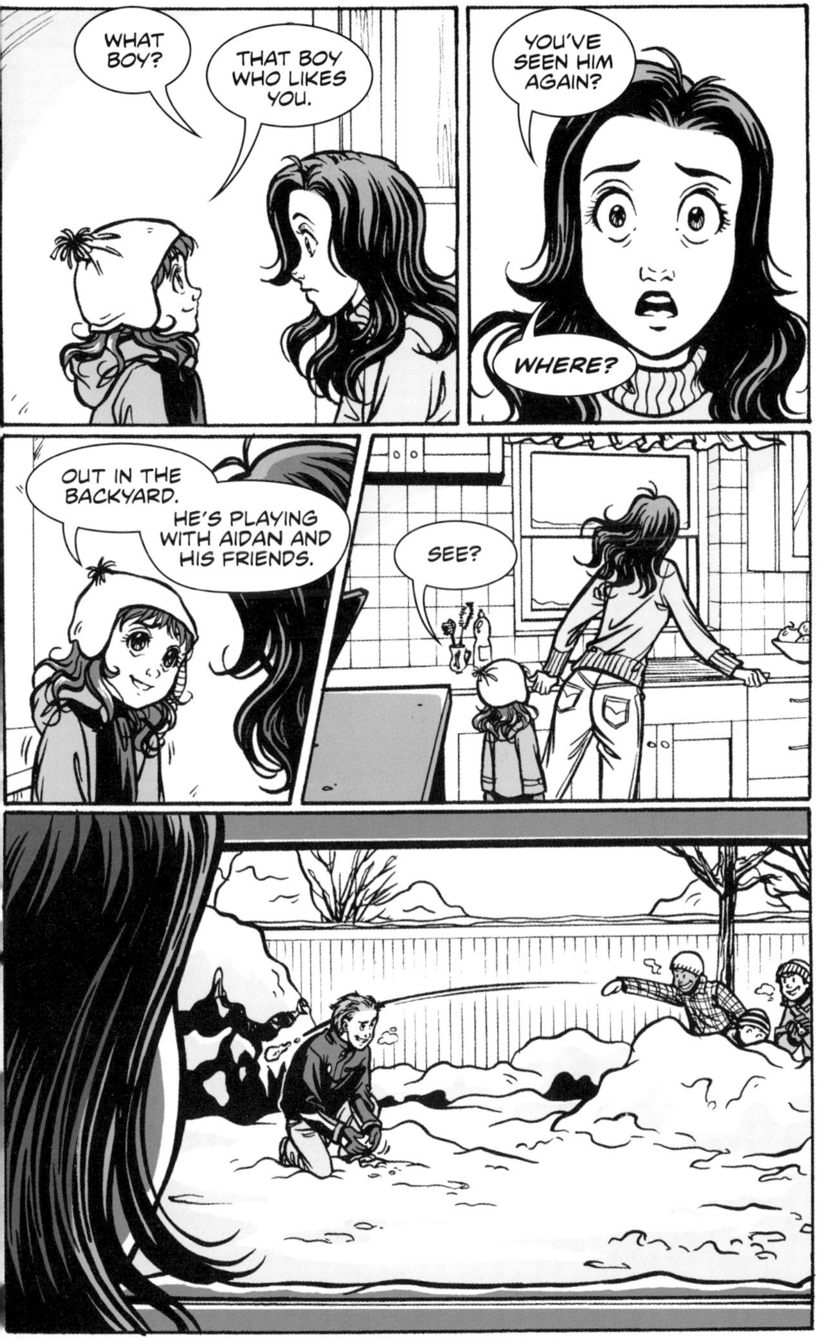
WHAT BOY?
THAT BOY WHO LIKES YOU.
YOU'VE SEEN HIM AGAIN?
WHERE?
OUT IN THE BACKYARD.
HE'S PLAYING WITH AIDAN AND HIS FRIENDS.
SEE?